"Fifteen Y...
And Your Father Took Me...,
Bella—Treated Me Like Family.
It's A Debt I've Never Forgotten.
And One I Intend To Repay."

He graced her with a slash of a smile. "You're welcome to stay as long as you want."

"That's a very generous thing to say. But you don't owe me anything. One night's stay is all I'll be—"

"We'll see about that," he interrupted. "We'll see what the doctor says tomorrow."

"All right, Michael," she said, too tired to argue. "But I don't want to take your room from you. I can move into a guest room or—"

"That's not necessary." His smoky gaze briefly scanned hers. "You look very comfortable right here in my bed."

Her eyes widened. *One night. Just one night.*

He regarded her for a moment; then he turned to leave.

"It's good to see you again," she called after him.

He paused in the doorframe but didn't look back. "It's good to see you, too, Bella."

Dear Reader,

'Tis the season to read six passionate, powerful and provocative love stories from Silhouette Desire!

Savor *A Cowboy & a Gentleman* (#1477), December's MAN OF THE MONTH, by beloved author Ann Major. A lonesome cowboy rekindles an old flame in this final title of our MAN OF THE MONTH promotion. MAN OF THE MONTH has had a memorable fourteen-year run and now it's time to make room for other exciting innovations, such as DYNASTIES: THE BARONES, a Boston-based Romeo-and-Juliet continuity with a happy ending, which launches next month, and—starting in June 2003—Desire's three-book sequel to Silhouette's out-of-series continuity THE LONE STAR COUNTRY CLUB. Desire's popular TEXAS CATTLEMAN'S CLUB continuity also returns in 2003, beginning in November.

This month DYNASTIES: THE CONNELLYS concludes with *Cherokee Marriage Dare* (#1478) by Sheri WhiteFeather, a riveting tale featuring a former Green Beret who rescues the youngest Connelly daughter from kidnappers. Award-winning, bestselling romance novelist Rochelle Alers debuts in Desire with *A Younger Man* (#1479), the compelling story of a widow's sensual renaissance. Barbara McCauley's *Royally Pregnant* (#1480) offers a fabulous finale to Silhouette's cross-line CROWN AND GLORY series, while a feisty rancher corrals the sexy cowboy-next-door in *Her Texas Temptation* (#1481) by Shirley Rogers. And a blizzard forces a lone wolf to deliver his hometown sweetheart's infant in *Baby & the Beast* (#1482) by Laura Wright.

Here's hoping you find all six of these supersensual Silhouette Desire titles in your Christmas stocking.

Enjoy!

Joan Marlow Golan

Joan Marlow Golan
Senior Editor, Silhouette Desire

Please address questions and book requests to:
Silhouette Reader Service
U.S.: 3010 Walden Ave., P.O. Box 1325, Buffalo, NY 14269
Canadian: P.O. Box 609, Fort Erie, Ont. L2A 5X3

Baby & the Beast
LAURA WRIGHT

Silhouette®
Desire®

Published by Silhouette Books
America's Publisher of Contemporary Romance

SILHOUETTE BOOKS

ISBN 0-373-76482-0

BABY & THE BEAST

Copyright © 2002 by Laura Wright

This edition published by arrangement with Harlequin Books S.A.

Visit Silhouette at www.eHarlequin.com

Printed in U.S.A.

Books by Laura Wright

Silhouette Desire

Cinderella & the Playboy #1451
Hearts Are Wild #1469
Baby & the Beast #1482

LAURA WRIGHT

has spent most of her life immersed in the world of acting, singing and competitive ballroom dancing. But when she started writing romance, she knew she'd found the true desire of her heart! Although born and raised in Minneapolis, Laura has also lived in New York City, Milwaukee and Columbus, Ohio. Currently, she is happy to have set down her bags and made Los Angeles her home. And a blissful home it is—one that she shares with her theatrical production manager husband, Daniel, and three spoiled dogs. During those few hours of downtime from her beloved writing, Laura enjoys going to art galleries and movies, cooking for her hubby, walking in the woods, lazing around lakes, puttering in the kitchen and frolicking with her animals. Laura would love to hear from you. You can write to her at P.O. Box 5811 Sherman Oaks, CA 91413 or e-mail her at laurawright@laurawright.com.

To my wonderful editor, Stephanie Maurer—
here's to our beloved "Beasts!"

One

Snow fell relentlessly from a gunmetal-gray sky, coating the naked trees with an icy frosting.

Isabella Spencer pulled her wool hat down over her ears, trying to ignore the wintry glaze forming on the scarf that covered her neck and mouth. Pushing back a mounting sense of worry, she closed the door on the remaining warmth inside her lifeless car and stepped out onto the deserted road. She was two hours outside Minneapolis—and thirty miles from the small town she wanted so desperately to return to.

But fate seemed to have other ideas.

It was barely November, yet the frigid morning wind whipped at her face like tiny knives, batting her from side to side as though she were nothing more than a crumpled ball of newspaper.

Flares. Go get the flares. Someone will be by soon.
Her center of gravity newly broadened by several inches, she trudged carefully through a foot of snow to the trunk of her car, cursing the imbeciles at the weather station for their false predictions, cursing her cell phone with its short-lived battery. And as she rooted out several orange flares, lit them and laid them in the snow, she cursed the car that her husband had assured her was in fine working order.

Of course, that had been more than seven months ago. Before Rick had left her for the freedom divorce provided, before he'd gotten drunk, plowed into a telephone pole and died just a few hours later.

The shiver that ran through her had nothing to do with the cold this time. Her husband was gone. He hadn't wanted her and he hadn't wanted the child growing inside her, and the sooner she put that stinging piece of knowledge behind her the better. She was going home, back to Fielding, to start a new life with the new year. And she'd be damned if she was going to let a snowstorm and ghosts from the past stop her.

As the now familiar jabs of pain invaded her hips, then shot downward, Isabella slipped back inside her car, being careful of her protruding belly. The car's interior was only slightly warmer than outside, but at least she was free of the raw wind. Whatever had caused her car to break down had nothing to do with the battery, thank God. She turned the key and switched the heat to high. The delicious warmth that shot from the vents could only last for a few minutes, she reminded herself. Then she'd have to turn it off, conserve as much as she could for as long as she could.

"It's okay, sweetie," Isabella cooed, laying a hand on her belly. "I won't let anything happen to you."

Her child gave a healthy kick, urging its mother to ignore the chill in her chest and legs and the scratch of what felt like icicles in her throat. She would fight for warmth. She would fight for her child.

Her gaze lifted. First to heaven, asking her late father for help, then lower to the windshield. Snow pelted the glass, shutting her off from the outside world one perfect snowflake at a time.

Michael Wulf glanced out the tinted rearside window of the town car whisking him home from the airport. Beyond the car's warm borders, the wind roared, causing the car to pitch slightly.

Just yesterday he'd been in Los Angeles, chuckling at the paltry first offer he'd received from Micronics to purchase a prototype of his vocal-command software. The heads of corporations never fully understood whom they were dealing with when they first met with him. They'd heard rumors that he was a mystery, a hermit, a genius, but they were never certain how to play the game.

Michael taught them quickly enough.

He'd finally left the warm sunshine with a very profitable deal closed, returning home to freezing temperatures. But the early-season snowstorm that met his plane wasn't an unwelcome sight. He appreciated Minnesota and its climate, valued the hibernation, the solitude, the solace. Although he did miss the long daylight hours now that the beginnings of winter were here.

It was only early afternoon and yet the gray sky and unrelenting snowfall had turned the surrounding landscape dim. It was hard to see fifty feet in front of the car. But even with the hazardous conditions and his position in the back seat, Michael's gaze caught sight of a faint orange light glowing against the snow in the distance. And near it, on the side of the road, something resembling an igloo with side mirrors and an Illinois license plate sat in ice-coated silence.

"What the hell is that?" he muttered.

The driver slowed, glancing to his right. "Looks like an abandoned car, sir."

Abandoned. That word fisted around Michael's gut, warning him that things weren't always as they seemed. It would take all of five seconds to see if the car truly was abandoned. Five seconds he was willing to risk even in such a blizzard. "Stop."

The driver did as he was instructed, pulling over in front of the car. In a flash, Michael was out the door, his bad leg stiffening in the cold as he trekked the few feet to the car. But he hardly noticed the dull ache. He was alert as he swept several inches of snow from the window, intent to see for himself that no one remained inside.

Suddenly his breath came out in a rush of fog. A woman sat in the driver's seat. She was bundled from head to foot in down and wool, asleep—or at least he hoped she was asleep.

"Miss? Miss? Can you hear me?" He yanked open the door and ripped off his glove, then bent down and dipped a hand inside her scarf. A strong, steady pulse beat against his fingers.

She stirred then, her eyes fluttering open. She stared up at him with large, deep-blue orbs that, though shrouded with uncertainty, spoke directly to his soul.

Deep-blue windows he'd seen somewhere before.

Her lips parted. "You found me."

And that voice. It was scratchy and raw, but he knew that voice.

The snow swirled around him like an ominous cyclone. Michael quickly shoved aside the questions forming in his mind. He needed to get her out of the car and to safety. But where? The hospital was forty-five minutes away. Too far.

"The heater stopped working...maybe half hour ago," she said softly, slowly. "I must've fallen asleep."

"You're damn lucky," he said, easing her out of the car then helping her to stand. "Another half hour and..." *And that car would've become an arctic tomb.* He didn't say it.

The wind burned his face and neck as he stripped off his coat and covered her. "You're going to be fine. Hang on."

"All right," she whispered.

He picked her up and started toward the town car just as the driver rushed up beside him to help.

"Sir, would you like me to carry—"

Michael ignored the offer. "Turn the heat on high and get us home as quickly as you can."

The man nodded. "Yes, sir."

Once tucked safely inside the car, Michael stripped off the woman's boots and rubbed her cold toes.

"Feels good," she said. "Itchy, but good."

After her feet were warm, he slid off her gloves and rubbed her small hands between his large ones. Then he gathered her in his arms and held her close.

"How long were you out there?" he asked.

The woman let her head fall against his shoulder as she answered with a sigh, "Since ten. This morning."

Five hours.

He cursed softly. "Just try to relax. You're safe now." Although a trace disoriented, she was going to be okay, he knew it somehow. But still, deep worry pricked at him. Her padded down coat couldn't hide what he could feel against his side.

"When's your baby due?" he asked.

She looked at him. "About a month."

His jaw tightened. What idiot would let his wife travel alone through a snowstorm at this stage of her pregnancy? Well, he was sure going to find out.

With gentle precision, he drew off her scarf. He'd been so intent on getting her to shelter, he hadn't been able to take a good look at her until now—except for her incredible and very familiar eyes. And what he could see made his chest tighten. Long waves of pale blond hair, heart-shaped face and a soft mouth. Again familiarity rapped at his mind. How the devil did he know her? He rarely went to social events, never went into town.

"Thank you," she mumbled, letting her head fall back onto his shoulder again. "Thank you for coming to get me, Michael."

At that, he froze like the icicles hanging off the stand of trees they passed. His mind worked, sharp and quiet, feeding information piece by piece until an answer formed.

And what an answer it was.

Falling asleep beside him sat the girl—no, the woman. A very pregnant woman. And the one person on earth to whom he owed a debt. One he'd vowed to pay back a long time ago.

He grabbed his cell phone, pushed a button and uttered, "Dr. Pinta," into the receiver.

The old doctor who had treated three generations of Fielding residents and was as close to a friend as Michael allowed himself to have picked up on the second ring.

"I need you, Thomas."

Visions of hot chocolate and electric blankets danced in Isabella's fuzzy head. Along with a grainy movie of her childhood crush dressed in shining armor, rescuing her from a white dragon who breathed hail, instead of fire. It was lovely, but the closer she got to the chocolate and blankets and handsome knight, the more her toes itched and her throat hurt.

"Isabella?"

The voice came from far away, through a snow-covered haze.

"Isabella, I need you to wake up."

The tone was parental and she forced her eyes to open and focus. She could feel that she was fully dressed, see that she was covered by several blankets and in a room that was not her own.

As she glanced around, her heart thumped madly in her chest. The room was large and furnished in dark wood. Drawn curtains made up the wall in front of her, a fire roared and crackled to her left, and a man sat beside her. A man she recognized instantly. His balding head, scholarly gray beard and hook nose gave him away.

Dr. Pinta's kind eyes settled on her. "Well, we're very glad to see you, my dear. How are you feeling?"

Her mind whirled with thoughts and questions, but none more important than one. "My baby?"

"Your baby's just fine. And so are you." He smiled. "You were very smart to set out those flares."

Her hands went to her belly, felt the warmth, the life there, and she sighed with relief.

"It was a close call, but thank the good Lord someone came along in time," the doctor added.

The doctor glanced over his shoulder and Isabella followed his gaze. Sitting in a thronelike chair upholstered in emerald-green velvet, facing the fire, was a man. Something inside her, perhaps inside her heart, knew instantly that the knight in her dream had been no vision, after all.

As images flashed through her mind—snow glazing her car, the door opening to reveal her rescuer, lying against the solid wall of his chest—her knight met her gaze, firelight illuminating his steel-gray eyes, rumpled black hair and granitelike features.

"Hello, Bella."

Only two men had ever called her that. One was her father, Emmett, who had passed away almost fifteen years ago. And the other was the sixteen-year-old runaway from a boys' home in Minneapolis her father had taken in.

Even at the age of thirteen, Isabella had known that she loved that boy, with his quick mind and brusque nature—even with the limp that had roused teasing and taunting from other kids in town.

But she'd lost him after her father's death. The boy had left Fielding after her great-aunt had taken her in, but couldn't take him, too.

Michael Wulf.

The picked-on outcast who'd turned into the misunderstood genius. A celebrity. She'd kept track of his progress and had even thought of getting in touch with him when she'd read that he'd moved back to Fielding three years ago. But she'd been married by then and living in Chicago. She'd had to put every ounce of energy into saving her marriage, into trying to find out why her husband had changed from charming to disinterested the moment they'd said, "I do."

A curious smile found its way to her mouth. "Michael. Thank you."

He gave her a quick nod. "It was nothing."

"You saved my life. And my baby's. That's something."

"I'm just glad I was there."

He never *had* taken a compliment well. "So am I. I thought I was dreaming when I woke up and saw you. It's been such a long time."

His shadowed gaze moved over her, pausing at her belly. "A long time."

His voice was low and deep, but tender, and she was instantly taken back in time. The gruff kid who had never been gruff with her.

A smile curled through her. Michael Wulf had been the boy she'd wanted to give her first kiss to, her heart to. Lord, how time flew. Certainly enough for her to see—and sense—the difference in him. He'd grown handsomer in fifteen years, but those gray eyes that had once been angry and troubled were as hard as steel now.

She knew some of his past hurts, but whatever had happened after he'd disappeared from Fielding had left him far more scarred. And she wondered about it.

Dr. Pinta put a hand over hers. "Is there someone I can call for you, my dear?"

She shook her head. "No."

"Your husband?" Michael offered, the hard lines of his mouth deepening.

Isabella looked away, suddenly feeling very tired. "He died seven months ago."

"Oh, I *am* sorry," Doc said softly. "What about someone in Fielding? Anyone expecting you?"

When she'd married Rick four years ago, he'd urged her to cut the lines of communication with anyone in Fielding. It had practically broken her heart, but in an effort to save her marriage, she'd done as he'd asked. She had no idea what to expect when she returned home, no idea if her old friends would embrace her.

"I'm going to stay at the hotel for a week or so until I can get my father's store back in working order," she said. "I've decided to turn it into a pastry shop." She looked at Dr. Pinta, sensing she had to explain further. "I'm planning on living in the apartment above it. It'll be a perfect home for me and the baby—once it's cleaned up of course."

"We'll all be glad to have you back, my dear. And a pastry shop," Doc said with a slow grin. "Good, good. Are you going to be selling those cinnamon rolls of yours?"

She nodded, returning his friendly smile. "When do you think I can go—"

"I think you should stay right where you are," Michael said firmly.

Doc nodded. "I agree. You and the baby should rest." From his coat pocket came a loud beeping sound. He reached in, took out his beeper and stared at the message. "Good Lord, it's certainly a day for emergencies. Mrs. Dalton has had an accident, something about her hip.''

''I hope she'll be all right,'' Isabella offered, her mind scattered with the events of the day.

Doc looked up. ''Sorry, my dear, I need to go. I have to stop in town and get some supplies. The Dalton place is at least twenty miles out. I don't think I'll be able to come back until morning.''

Michael nodded. ''I'll take care of her, Thomas.''

An unfamiliar tug of awareness spread through Isabella at that simple promise. She grabbed for the doctor's hand. ''I don't want to put anyone out. I could go with you. The hotel is right on the—''

Doc Pinta stood up. ''No, no. The snow has let up quite a bit, but it's getting colder. I don't want you picking up another chill. Not in your condition.''

''She'll stay here,'' Michael stated firmly. ''I'll move my things into the guest room.''

Isabella felt her cheeks warm as she once again looked around the room. This time she noted several personal items: the silver watch that her father had given Michael for his sixteenth birthday on the nightstand, a book about solar-powered homes on a bench, aboriginal paintings on the walls and framed photographs on the mantel, each depicting what she imagined were Michael's ''children''—the high-tech interiors of cars, boats and houses.

This was *his* room, *his* bed.

Her pulse stumbled and the room suddenly compressed into a sort of tunnel with Michael Wulf at the end. Lord, she must have caught more than a chill.

Only a fever could make her childish crush seem in danger of turning into a full-fledged, grown-up one. She was in Fielding to start a new life, create a future for herself and her child, not return to teenage dreams from the past.

"I really can't stay here," Isabella said, hearing the ring of panic in her voice. How could she sleep in his bed, against his pillows, surrounded by the scent of him? "I need to be at my place. I have a cleaning crew coming from St. Cloud to help me get everything—"

"They won't make it out in weather like this, Isabella." Doc Pinta reached down and gave her hand a squeeze. "What you need to do is calm down. You're in no shape tonight to brave the elements. It's not good for the baby." He turned to Michael. "If anything changes, please call me."

Michael nodded. "Of course."

"You and that baby get some rest, young lady." Doc Pinta left the room, calling over his shoulder, "I'll see you first thing in the morning."

An unwelcome cloud of anxiety floated in the air just above Isabella's heart as she watched the doctor go—leaving her alone with the subject of her teenage dreams.

Dressed in simple but expensive black, Michael crossed to the bed, his limp more pronounced than she remembered. But that minor limitation hardly diminished his striking appearance and the commanding manner that burned around him like a living, breathing thing.

Up close he was even more fiercely handsome than she remembered. Dark, hooded eyes, sensual mouth, olive skin—he nearly took her breath away. He'd grown, well over six feet now with the body of a gladiator. Obviously his impediment hadn't stopped him from staying fit, she mused as a twinge of pain erupted in her lower back.

But though Michael had grown in stature and appearance, Isabella could feel the oppressive heat of the anger and the resentment he still carried. A weighty burden he looked unlikely to discard anytime soon.

"I want you to know that I really appreciate your putting me up," she told him. "I won't be a bother, I promise."

Michael's features tightened. "Fifteen years ago you and your father took me in, Bella, treated me like family. It's a debt I've never forgotten. And one I intend to repay." He graced her with a slash of a smile—something she imagined he didn't do very often. "I'm glad you're here, and you're welcome to stay as long as you want."

Her heart began to soften like clay in a warm palm, but she fought it. His voice was thoughtful, but the meaning was clear. He was offering her his home and his protection because he felt he owed her and her father.

"Thanks," she said with a calm she didn't feel. "That's a very generous thing to say. But you don't owe me anything. One night's stay is all I'll be—"

"We'll see about that," he interrupted, plowing a

hand through his hair. "We'll see what the doctor says tomorrow."

Just then, an arrow of pain shot into her lower back, making her wince. These little jolts were coming all too frequently the past few weeks. Her little one obviously wanted to see the world. *And Mommy can't wait to see you, my sweetie. Just give me a little longer.*

"All right, Michael," she said, too tired to argue something that sounded so reasonable no matter what his motivations were. "But I don't want to take your room from you. I can easily move into a guest room or—"

"That's not necessary." His smoky gaze briefly scanned hers. "You look very comfortable right here in my bed."

Her eyes widened and her breasts tightened. *One night. Just one night.*

"I won't have you moving," he said. "I'm going downstairs to make sure that Thomas is on his way. I'll bring you up some dinner. Soup sound all right?"

She nodded, grateful that he was going to leave for a while so she could breathe normally again. "Sounds perfect."

"My housekeeper only comes during the week, so we'll both have to suffer my cooking until tomorrow. Anything else you need?"

"A little sunshine would be great," she joked lamely.

He turned then and uttered the word "drapes," and

the wall of chestnut fabric in front of her parted to reveal floor-to-ceiling windows.

Isabella gasped, both at what seemed to be his magic and at the view. The dim bluish light of a late afternoon in early winter seeped into the room. Outside, she could see gnarled, leafless trees, a pond frozen over and acres and acres of white under a gray sky. To any true Midwesterner, it was a beautiful scene.

And Michael's amazing technology had brought it to her in one simple command. She'd certainly read about his inventions, just never seen one.

"Very impressive, Michael."

He shrugged. "It's actually a pretty simple process."

"Not to the technologically impaired. My VCR has been blinking 12:00 for a good decade."

"Well, I can't make a cinnamon roll. To me, that's impressive." He regarded her for moment, the cogs of his mind working behind his eyes, then he turned to leave.

"It's good to see you again," she called after him.

He paused at the door, but didn't look back. "It's good to see you, too, Bella."

Then he was gone, and the room felt cooler. Which was odd because his attitude and manner were not particularly warm.

She turned toward the fire. Why in the world did she feel so safe here, in his lair, his hideout from the world, as the media called it?

"The millionaire recluse who lives in an enormous

house of glass on thirty acres of woodland high above a sleepy town," she'd read. "Driven to levels of success that most mortals wouldn't dare strive for."

He was an enigma, they said. At thirty-one, Michael Wulf made the world wonder—about his personal history, as well as his extraordinarily profitable high-tech developments.

Though he seemed to have no past, he was truly a man of the future. He created houses with brains and cars that responded to vocal commands. But unlike others in his field, he had no taste for celebrity.

They also wrote that he had no wife, no family, few friends and a giant chip on his shoulder. They said that he walked with a limp. And they speculated that perhaps the lone wolf had once been caught in a trap.

But Isabella knew a truth that all those journalists who wrote about him would never know. How he'd been tossed away by his parents for a handicap he couldn't control and shoved into a boys' home. How he'd been treated by his peers for being different. How determined he'd been to rise above them all.

And it seemed that he'd succeeded. He did indeed live high above a sleepy little town, a town that had once rejected him. But in her opinion, living in hiding was no way to live.

She exhaled heavily, her hands moving to her belly. Perhaps it was this new nurturing side of her, but she wanted to help him, lift him out of that black hole that held him hostage. But somehow she knew that if she did, if she got close to him again, the odds of reviving that adolescent crush were great.

Not that her potential desires mattered. The boy from years ago had looked on her as a little girl, while the man today apparently looked on her as an unpaid debt.

Not to mention that you're eight months pregnant and resemble a beach ball.

She rubbed her stomach and said softly, "But I wouldn't have it any other way."

What she needed to do was concentrate on this new life she was carving out for herself: opening her pastry shop, creating a home, raising her child and putting the past to rest.

But rest appeared unlikely as long as she was under the same roof as that past: the very handsome and disturbing Michael Wulf.

Two

Michael leaned back in his armchair and took in the view.

Several feet away, Bella lay asleep in his massive bed, wrapped in the royal-blue robe he'd loaned her. She'd grown into a beautiful woman over the past decade, and her pregnancy only accentuated that beauty.

She hugged the down pillow like a lover, her face content, her tawny lashes brushing the tops of her cheekbones. And as the last flicker of red from the fire illuminated her long blond hair, he couldn't help but wonder if this angel from his past had been sent from heaven to torture him.

Tonight, however, he hadn't let himself spend enough time with her to find out. After Thomas had left, he'd gone down to the kitchen and opened a can of chicken soup, made some toast to go with it, then brought it up to her on a tray. She'd wanted him to stay and have dinner with her, but he'd declined.

He never ate with anyone. As a child, the chaos of living and eating with sixty hungry boys, of having to fight for every scrap of food, had made him yearn for solitude and peace. And he'd found them both out on the road when he'd finally escaped from Youngstown School.

Even when he'd come to Fielding, stayed with Bella and her father, his newfound independence had continued. Emmett would say something like ''A man has to have a little space,'' then hand Michael a plate of food and a glass of milk.

Emmett Spencer had been one in a million. Michael knew he would never forget how the man had taken him in, no questions asked, and acted as a father figure, a mentor, even taught him all about electronics. Then there was Bella, who had taught him about kindness and given him her friendship.

But tonight, Michael thought as he watched her, tonight, as he'd laid that dinner tray before her, he hadn't looked on her as a friend. He'd even contemplated making an exception to his dining rule. For her. And both of those realizations unnerved him. Unnerved him enough to cry ''work'' as an excuse and get the hell out of there.

Just then, Bella sighed in her sleep. Rubbing his jaw, Michael cursed softly. He'd never been a voyeur.

And he didn't have time to think about the past. There was work to be done and deals to be made.

But today, when he'd opened that car door, seen those eyes—held a very grown-up Bella against him in that car—an addictive warmth had seeped into his icy blood, making him want to stay put, hold on to her this time. And that sense of longing hadn't subsided one ounce in the hours since. Instead, it had seemed to grow.

Obviously she was potent acid to his ironwill, eating away at his resolve, and he knew that he'd better remember why she was here. Remember the only thing he wanted from her.

Acknowledgment of a debt paid in full.

So although his mind warned him to get out of this room, what was left of his sense of duty would not allow it. If she needed him for anything, he would be here.

On another soft, sleepy sigh, Isabella kicked the covers off her legs. The robe she wore lay open from toes to midthigh, and Michael couldn't help but catch a glimpse of those long, toned legs before he forced his gaze back to the dying fire.

He slid his heel along the rug and stretched out his leg. The damn thing hurt tonight. More than usual. But he fought the pain head-on, always had. At three when he'd taken a tumble down the basement steps and broken his leg, he'd been as brave as a three-year-old could be. When the simple break had damaged a nerve and turned into a not-so-simple life-long affliction, he'd held his own. And even when his parents couldn't handle raising a crippled child and had abandoned him to the state's foster-care system, he'd done his best to take care of himself and get on with it.

Flinching slightly, he stood up and walked over to the window, gritting his teeth as he shoved the ache away. The break in the snow this afternoon had been fleeting. Outside a storm of white raged against the night sky, glazing the trees, blanketing the earth as far as he could see. And it showed no signs of stopping.

It would be a miracle if Thomas made it out to the house tomorrow. What Michael had imagined to be a couple of days caring for Bella to pay back an old debt was beginning to look as if it could stretch into a week.

His gut tightened. Why did that worry him so much? He didn't have to see her except to bring her meals, watch over her at night.

Pushing away from the window, he went to stand beside the bed. Damn, she was beautiful. And harmless and pregnant and... *And what, Wulf? What is it? What's she doing to you?*

The devil's response hung in the air as he covered her with the blanket she'd kicked off, then returned to his chair by the fire.

Bella made him feel...alive.

By five o'clock the following afternoon, Isabella had one bad case of cabin fever.

All hopes of being released from Michael Wulf's

hideout and the heat of Michael Wulf's gaze had disappeared the moment she'd woken up that morning and seen God's endless shower of snow. The cleaning crew had been canceled, Doc Pinta hadn't been able to come, and neither had the housekeeper. Isabella and Michael were alone, trapped by a blizzard that showed no signs of ending.

Ever the gentleman, Michael had brought her some magazines that his housekeeper had left behind and, of course, two square meals. But he never stayed, and she was growing increasingly weary of reading about secret celebrity hideaways and the world's largest pan of lasagna.

What she needed was a respite from rest.

She wrapped the terry-cloth robe tighter around her—the robe that held the faint scent of spicy male to it—and headed for the door.

Fortunately, when Doc Pinta had phoned that morning, he'd told her that if she felt strong enough, she could get out of bed for a bit. And that was just what she intended to do.

Snug in a pair of Michael's large wool socks, she stepped out into the hallway—a glass hallway suspended ten feet above the ground to be exact. Isabella glanced around, feeling a little off balance, not unusual considering her center of gravity had shifted considerably over the past few months.

Twilight came early at this time of year and even earlier in a storm, so the passage was dim. It appeared unlit, but that quickly changed the moment she took a wary step into it. Apparently the floor was pressure sensitive, because for each step she took, another section of hallway lit up.

Isabella just stared, openmouthed. How could she help it? It wasn't just the glowing floor that impressed her, it was the view the hallway presented. On either side of her lay acres of snowy woodland, and over her head, a blanket of thick white covered the glass ceiling.

Extraordinary.

It was with great regret that she left the hallway at its end and entered a large room with a marble floor, a grand piano and a jungle of plants surrounding an elevator.

An elevator that stood open, waiting.

She took a deep breath and looked around her. Okay, Michael probably wouldn't love her poking around his house unaccompanied. But he was obviously too busy with his work to entertain guests. If she looked at it that way, she was helping him out by entertaining herself, right?

With that bit of warped logic to fuel her quest, she moseyed into the silver cylinder. She could do a little exploring, then be back in her room by the time Michael brought dinner. No harm done.

But she wasn't going anywhere, she quickly realized. Because as she glanced around, she noticed that there were no buttons to push anywhere.

"All right," she said, touching the smooth walls. "First things first. How do I make this door close?"

Isabella gasped as the door closed instantly.

"I guess that's the way," she muttered. "Now, I

suppose saying the word 'up' would be just too easy.''

The elevator didn't move.

''That's what I thought.''

She tried a few synonyms for the word up, but nothing happened. She tried the words *guest, Michael, Wulf* and *Fielding*. Still the elevator remained immobile.

As she racked her brain for a more clever answer to this riddle, a wrench of pain shot across her lower back. She arched, stretching a little, then settled both hands on her belly and rubbed. ''Are you as frustrated as Mommy, sweetie? Or are you just ready to meet the world and see your new home—''

At that the elevator shot upward. Stunned, Isabella gripped the steel railing to hold her steady and tried to remember the last word she'd uttered.

Home.

An interesting choice.

And one she never would've thought of.

The elevator came to a smooth stop at what she guessed was the top of the house, and the doors slid open. Cautiously she stepped out into a room bathed in bright yellow light. It was an office. And what Michael deemed home.

''Michael,'' she called out tentatively, ''you here?''

There was no answer, and she walked into the room, her gaze riveted on the scenery before her. Constructed primarily of glass and steel, the turret-shaped room boasted hardwood floors covered in tan rugs, two worn brown leather couches, a state-of-the-art workout contraption, a massive television and stereo system, and two arcade-size, freestanding video games.

For just a moment, her gaze rested on the video games. It warmed her heart to see them and to know that her father's influence on Michael had remained.

She walked farther into the circular space toward the massive desk, which held two computers, a fax machine and a printer. She noted the clutter there, as well—stacks of paper, disks, files, pens and pencils.

She would never have guessed it, but stern, rigid Michael Wulf was a messy guy.

She chuckled at the thought just as her gaze caught on a framed drawing just above the desk. It was an etching, very old, but in fine condition. It was a scene from the fairy tale "Rumplestiltskin." And at different points on the wall were more etchings of other fairy tales: "Sleeping Beauty," "The Princess and the Pea," "The Nightingale," "The Ugly Duckling."

"What are you doing?"

She whirled around to see Michael emerge from the elevator, looking drop-dead sexy in a dark-gray sweater and black jeans, his jaw tight, his eyes dark as thunderclouds.

"What am I doing in here?" she asked innocently. "Or out of bed?"

"Both."

"I was going a little stir-crazy," she said, smiling into his glower. "You know, locked up in the tower?"

His brow rose. "Obviously you weren't locked in well enough."

She touched her belly. "We're both a little weary of being cooped up."

His eyes softened as he looked at her stomach. "I understand that, but you really should be resting. What happened to doctor's orders?"

"He said I could take a walk if I felt up to it."

Michael didn't move from his spot in front of the elevator. "I don't allow people up here, Bella."

"Not even to clean or—"

"I do that myself."

She glanced at the desk with its overflowing mess and grinned. "So I see."

With something close to a growl, he stepped back into the elevator and motioned for her to follow. "All right. Let's go. Back downstairs and off your feet."

"I could sit," she suggested. The twinge running up her spine heartily agreed.

"You came way too close to having hypothermia yesterday, Bella."

"That's a little overly dramatic, don't you think?"

"What I think is that I'm not taking any chances. I'm going to walk you down—"

"Wait, please. It's nice up here. The view." She laughed. "The clutter."

He glared at her.

"Okay, okay," she muttered dejectedly.

She must've pulled off one great downcast expression, because he breathed an impatient sigh and said,

"How about we go into the kitchen? You can sit down and relax while I make you some dinner."

"How about you make *us* some dinner?" she suggested as she walked toward him.

"We'll see."

"That expression is beginning to annoy me." She stepped into the elevator and tried to ignore the woodsy scent of him.

He mumbled, "Second floor," and they descended.

Shaking her head, she said, "I wouldn't have started with anything that easy."

He turned to look at her, his brow arched. "By the way, how did you manage to get up there?"

She smiled. "I stumbled on the password."

"No more stumbling," he warned.

"But—"

"No buts, either."

She placed her hands on what used to be her hips. "You know, you're not supposed to argue with a pregnant woman."

"Who says?" The look he tossed her was somewhere between irritated and interested.

"It's in the book of pregnancy rules."

"And the author of that book is…"

"Gosh, can't remember."

The elevator stopped and the door opened. "That's convenient."

Laughing, she followed him through the jungle room, past a small dining room and then into a large, open-air kitchen with beamed ceilings.

Much like the other rooms in Michael's house, the

kitchen boasted floor-to-ceiling windows that left you nose to nose with the hillside and snowy landscape, separated only by glass. All the appliances were black and very modern. No buttons or dials. And she couldn't help but wonder just how long it had taken his housekeeper to remember the vocal commands for everything.

But the most interesting thing in the room was happening on top of the center island. Under several glass domes and UV light, herbs grew hydroponically. The setup was incredibly progressive with a small computer attached to each dome. She could actually read the internal temperature and how many hours, minutes and seconds the herbs needed to mature.

It was little wonder that Michael was a millionaire, she thought as she sat down at a green glass table.

She was getting a little tired, and those pricking pains in her back were intensifying. But little twinges were expected in the last month of pregnancy. She just needed a good soak in the tub. Maybe after dinner.

"You know," she began, arching her back a few times, "that book I mentioned also states quite clearly that all pregnant women should receive chocolate-chip ice cream once a day followed by an hour-long foot massage."

He poured her a glass of milk and set it down in front of her. "And husbands actually buy this?"

Her heart tripped awkwardly. "The book or what's in it?"

"Either."

"If they love their wives enough, I guess," she said softly, taking a swallow of the cold milk.

Michael began to assemble a sandwich. "Did your husband own a copy of that book?"

A profound sadness poured through Isabella. Michael probably thought that she and Rick had had a great relationship, typical loving husband and wife. And why wouldn't he? She was pregnant, after all.

She glanced up at Michael. "I don't imagine he did."

"I wasn't thinking, Bella," he said, expelling a breath. "It's none of my business. I'm sorry."

"No, don't be sorry." She took another swallow of milk, trying to think what to say next. For so long, she'd had to pretend that her marriage was a loving union, that her husband was content and satisfied with his life and with her. But she just couldn't lie anymore. "Rick didn't really want to be a husband. I think I was a challenge to him. The last virgin in Minnesota or something. So once he had me, once that wedding night was over..." She shrugged, heat creeping up her neck and dispersing into her cheeks.

Michael's fierce stare was unyielding as he finished her sentence. "He forgot just how lucky he was?"

She smiled. "Something like that. I kept trying, though. You know, I came from a family that stuck together through thick and not-so-thick."

"Yeah, I know."

Beneath his words, Isabella detected a hint of longing, but she wouldn't press him. "Well, Rick wanted a reason to leave, and when I told him I was pregnant he had one.''

''You weren't trying to have a baby?''

She shook her head. ''It just happened.'' She smiled as she rubbed her stomach. ''After he left, I felt so unbelievably angry. I held on to that anger for a while, then I realized that it wasn't healthy for me or the baby, so little by little I let it go. As easy as it would've been, I don't hate him for his weakness of character.''

''Well, you're a better person than me.'' Michael brought her the turkey sandwich he'd made, but he didn't sit down. just stood against the counter. ''I hate him and I never even met him. He left you, Bella.''

''Yes. But look at what he left me with.'' Grinning, she touched her stomach.

He nodded, then looked away.

Isabella took a bite of the sandwich and switched gears. ''Where did you go after you left Fielding? I always wanted to know.''

He paused, and she wondered if he was going to open up to her the way she just had with him. After all, it was a safe subject. But he didn't reply. ''Michael, if you don't—''

''Minneapolis,'' he said, opening a drawer on the outside of the fridge and grabbing a beer. ''I went to Minneapolis.''

''And what did you do there? I mean, you were only sixteen.''

''I was old enough to take care of myself.'' He popped the top of the beer and took a swallow. ''I used the skills your father taught me. You know, even though he worked on video games, the things he showed me opened my mind to what was possible. And opened doors for me in ways I couldn't have imagined.'' He paused to take another swallow of beer. "That's why I owe him.''

She had to ask. "And why do you owe me?''

"Let's just say that you were my guardian angel, Bella.''

Lord, she didn't want to be his angel. "Look, Michael, you don't owe either one of us anything. We both did what we did because we cared about you. Not because we were looking for a payoff later on.''

"Everyone wants a payoff.''

She shook her head. "You don't believe that.''

"Yes, I do.'' He opened the fridge and started rifling through it. "Whether the payoff is emotional, physical or monetary, everybody expects one.''

"Maybe that's true of some people, but...'' Her words trailed off as the dull pain in her back suddenly shot down her hips. She sucked in a breath of air and let it out slowly as the pain eased. What she really needed to do was finish her sandwich and go take that bath.

"Well, you've done enough for me,'' she said finally. "And as soon as this storm clears, we'll call it even, all right?''

"We'll see.''

She rolled her eyes as she scooped up her sandwich. "Michael, I swear if you say that one more time...''

Something was happening. It wasn't just eight-month pangs or Braxton Hicks contractions. Fire-crackers were erupting in her abdomen, shooting what felt like shards of broken cut glass to every corner of her body. Her sandwich fell to the floor as she leaned over, gripping her belly as another spear of pain drove down her spine, through her hips and circled her belly.

Michael was at her side in seconds. "What's wrong? What is it?"

"I need to go—" She gasped.

"Where do you need to go? Back to bed?"

She shook her head. "No. To the hospital. I need to go to the hospital." She glanced up at him, her breath catching in her throat as she felt the pain rising again like a gigantic wave set to crash. "The baby's coming."

Three

The steadfast control that Michael prided himself on threatened to snap. Bella's water had broken and she was in labor. The phone lines had gone down sometime in the afternoon, and his long driveway was knee-deep with snow.

Everything he normally relied on was of no use to him. No cell-phone service—his satellite hookup was worthless in this type of weather—and as he'd designed his home for hibernation, he had no snowmobile.

Which meant there was no way to get her into town.

What they did have, however, were Bella's pregnancy book, Michael's encyclopedias and three backup generators.

For the first time in a long time, he had to rely on instinct, not technology, and it felt completely foreign. But he'd be damned if he was going to let Bella know that.

After several long and very tense minutes, he'd gotten her back in bed, lay several clean towels beneath her, then rounded up some cool water, hot water, scissors, string, washcloths, more clean towels and sheets. He read as much as he could between her contractions. And when the pain gripped her, and she cried out, he tried to comfort her. Never letting her know that the sight and sound of her labor shook him to his very core.

He was lighting a fire when her soft voice broke through his thoughts. "Michael?"

He crossed to the bed and knelt down beside her.

"There's no way to get me to the hospital, right?" she said, her eyes filled with unease.

"No. I'm sorry."

She turned away from him then. Her jaw was set, her eyes glazed as she looked straight ahead, apparently concentrating. On what, he wasn't sure. But he wasn't going to ask any stupid questions.

"Can I get you anything? Ice chips? Juice?"

She shook her head. "Don't go anywhere."

"I'm not going anywhere." Dammit, he had to pull this off, had to keep her safe.

Her eyes suddenly shut, and her hands fisted the sheet. Beads of sweat broke out on her forehead, and she gave a cry of agony that made him want to put his fist through a wall, feel a little of the pain she was feeling.

But instead, he did the practical thing. He rinsed out a washcloth and wiped her face and neck, whispering words of encouragement, assuring her that everything would be all right.

Finally she released an enormous breath and her head dropped to one side.

"How are you feeling?" It was one of those stupid questions he hadn't wanted to utter, but his worry superseded good sense.

She turned to look at him, her eyes large and heavy with fatigue. "Like someone's trying to drive a truck through my abdomen."

He smiled at her and she put on a brave smile of her own.

She was something else.

Back in the boys' home, he'd seen many kids get hurt, sometimes staffers too. Hell, the gardener had practically sliced off his finger cleaning the lawn mower. The man had cried for three hours.

And Bella was actually making jokes, fighting through every bolt of pain with all she had.

"I have to tell you something." She reached for his hand, and he grabbed hold.

"What is it?"

"I'm really scared, Michael."

Without thinking, he brought her hand to his mouth and kissed it lightly. "I know."

"The baby's a month early."

"The baby is going to be perfect." Never in his

life had he felt so humbled—or so helpless. "We're going to do this together. Okay?"

"Okay." Her eyes drifted closed and her breathing slowed. "Distract me. Tell me something."

"Anything."

"Tell me about that day."

"What day, Bella?"

"When…when you first came to town. When you came to Fielding." She squeezed his hand. "The day you left that horrible place."

Michael hesitated. He'd disclosed the practicalities of his past to Bella and her father, but the details had been off-limits to everyone, including himself. The nightmare of the night he'd run away and the salvation he'd run to was something he'd vowed never to revisit. But right now, for Bella, he knew he'd recall both. He'd do anything to ease her mind and her fears.

His throat was dry as dust as he spoke. "I left Youngstown School at two o'clock on a Monday morning with fifty cents in my pocket and only the clothes on my back. I walked for about fifteen miles until I was too tired to go on. So I sat on the side of the road with my thumb out and waited."

Michael glanced down at her, saw that she was a little more relaxed than she'd been a moment ago and continued. "It was summer and hot—I'd sweated right through my T-shirt. And I remember being surprised that someone had actually stopped to pick me up."

Bella smiled and said softly, "With that sweaty T-shirt, I'll bet it was a girl, right?"

He chuckled. "It was a woman in her seventies."

"Seventy or seven—" her face tightened and she sucked in a breath "—teen?"

"Don't talk, Bella," he whispered. "Just breathe."

She whimpered, writhing on the bed, clutching his hand as another contraction clamped her body. The power of it shocked him. "Everything's all right. You're going to be fine. You're going to be a mother soon."

At that, she opened her eyes and looked up at him. He felt his heart squeeze as an expression of pure pleasure radiated from her eyes.

"I *can* do this," she said, biting her lip.

He nodded. "Of course you can."

Within seconds, the storm cloud passed over her face and she let out a sigh. "So…the…woman picked you up, and…and then what?"

He wiped her face with the cool cloth. "I'd bought a bruised banana from the gas station and it was all I'd had for breakfast, so I was starving. The woman had these homemade biscuits in her air-conditioned car, and the smell nearly drove me insane. I remember she told me to take as many as I wanted." He smiled as he began to massage her shoulder with his free hand. "I ate the whole lot and felt guilty as hell. But she said she didn't mind."

"Is that when you knew?" Bella whispered.

"Knew what?"

"That your luck was about to change?"

He thought about that for a moment. Luck wasn't a word in his vocabulary—he'd never really believed in the concept of luck. But then again... "I think I knew that my luck had changed the moment I stepped foot in the Fielding dime store and those kids were calling me—" his throat almost closed "—a cripple and peg leg."

Only the sounds of their breathing and the crackle of the fire could be heard until Bella whispered, "And then I came by with my water gun."

Memories burned in his mind. "You sure did. Shot those boys dead center."

A weary laugh escaped her. "They all looked like they'd just wet their pants."

Michael smiled, remembering the look of horror on those cruel young faces—and the triumph on little Bella's as she'd held her water pistol aloft like a .57 magnum. Maybe she was right. Was it actually possible that luck existed and that it had reached him? "That was a good day."

"Yeah." The look she sent him was soul-searching. "I'm really glad you're here."

It was as if someone had shot an arrow through his chest, jabbing his heart. Bella was counting on him to deliver this baby safely and into her arms. He wasn't going to let her down. His life was built on conquering challenges. Tonight, he was moving from high-tech to human whether he liked it or not.

He watched as her face contorted with pain once again, then listened as she groaned and whimpered. He didn't know much, but he did know they were getting close.

The baby was coming soon.

And he hoped to God he could make both the child and its mother proud tonight.

Night faded into dawn.

The pain was almost unimaginable, and all the control that Isabella had willed herself to possess had faded away. She felt close to collapse. But she refused to give up or give in.

She felt this overwhelming sense of connection with her child. Different and farther-reaching than even the bond she'd felt in the last months of pregnancy. She and her little one were finally ready to meet.

"I need a good solid push, Bella."

Michael glanced up at her, his own brow wet with sweat, his eyes just as determined as she felt. He'd read her pregnancy book and his encyclopedia with diligence, emerging with strength and confidence. She felt no embarrassment with him. His willingness to do whatever it took to bring this baby, whatever it took to make Isabella feel comfortable, made her feel so close to him, so trusting.

"Take a deep breath, Bella," he said, his tone insistent, "and give me everything you got."

Isabella raised herself on her elbows, filled her lungs with air and pushed. A distressed scream escaped her, and she bit her lip, tasted blood. Her knees shook. She felt as if she was being ripped apart.

"That's good," Michael told her. "One more time. Breathe in deep and—"

"Michael, if something happens to me..." she gasped.

His tone was fierce. "Nothing's going to happen to you while I'm around, you understand?"

It was as if time hadn't passed. All Michael's anger had evaporated, and their connection, their reliance on each other, had returned. But this time, it was she who needed his strength.

"Push, Bella," he demanded. "Push hard."

Arching her back, she gulped air and bore down. Through the grunts, the struggle, the sweat, her mind thrashed with worry. Could she do this? The bolts of pain fought with her good sense. Did every woman feel this awful press of panic?

Her breath came out on a sigh just as Michael said, "Oh, God, Bella."

"What?" she cried. "What's wrong?"

"Nothing's wrong," Michael assured her. "I can see the head." Awe, pure reverence filled his voice. "Do you think you can give me one more push?"

All fear left her in that moment. And as the morning wind howled outside and the snow fell by the bucketful, Bella fought for her baby, running on pure adrenaline and anticipation. Gripping the towels in her fists, eyes clamped shut, she inhaled deeply and bore down.

"That's it. That's it, Bella."

Isabella cried out as her child came into the world, their wails intermingled. Collapsing back against the pillows, she smiled weakly, listening to the high-pitched squall of her baby—sweet, miracle-making music.

"Bella?"

She opened her eyes then and saw Michael, his

eyes filled with happiness and amazement, holding her baby. "It's a girl."

A girl, Isabella silently repeated, her eyes filling with tears as she stared at the tiny infant that had come from her body and her soul.

Michael was stunned. Not just because he'd delivered this sweet little girl, but because he'd been here to see what a mother in love with her child looked like.

After he cut the cord and cleaned up the baby, he wrapped her in a towel until she looked like a big burrito. Then he handed the baby to her mother, who cooed and smiled and laughed, and cradled the tiny girl to her breast.

And Michael watched it all.

After a few minutes Bella met his gaze and smiled. "Thank you."

Thank *you* for letting me be a part of it, he wanted to say, but didn't. He was too filled with emotions he didn't recognize.

"You were amazing, Michael Wulf," she said.

"So were you," he said, his gaze fixed on hers. "What are you going to name her?"

She glanced down at the little cherub face. "I was thinking about Emily."

"After your dad?" Emmett would've been so proud of her, he thought as he watched her cuddle her child.

She nodded. "What do you think?

The question startled him. It wasn't something that he had any right to think about.

She touched his hand. "I really want your opinion. You helped bring her into the world."

He shook his head. "This was all you, Bella."

"I don't buy that and neither does Emily," she said with a tired smile.

He looked down at the baby, with her amazing blue eyes. Of course, most babies had blue eyes when they were born, but they didn't all have such an adorable expression or such a beautiful mother.

He couldn't stop the smile that broke across his face. Dammit, he hadn't done this much smiling in his whole life. "I think it's a perfect name for a perfect little girl," he acquiesced gruffly.

Bella glowed with pride. "She is perfect, isn't she?"

Michael just stood there, watching them, wonder coursing through his veins. But when mother and child yawned with fatigue he forced his emotion back and returned to work mode.

After a mild flurry of post-birth cleanup and fresh sheets, Emily's and Bella's eyes drifted closed, long lashes resting against contented faces.

He walked over to the fire, his leg knotted with pain, and fell into his chair. Of all the things he'd accomplished in his life, bringing little Emily into the world and placing her in her mother's arms was his greatest achievement.

And he knew that nothing would ever come close to rivaling it.

Four

The storm raged from morning into the gloomy darkness of afternoon. But Isabella awoke from a much-needed nap feeling only warm and safe and content. Sure, her muscles were slow, and everything below her neck felt stiff and sore, but she'd never felt happier.

And it was all because just a few hours ago, she'd become a mother.

The thought continued to make her smile, not to mention make her forget where she was. She honestly didn't care if the snow ever let up or if she ever left Michael's glass house or if her pastry shop had Christmas buns before Christmas—she just wanted to hang on to this incredible moment in time for as long as it would allow. Although she would've welcomed

Doc Pinta's agreement that her motherly instincts were right—that everything was just as it should be. But she would have to wait a day or two for that.

Emily fussed in her arms, and Isabella rocked her and cooed sweet words—true words. Her blue-eyed bundle responded instantly, blowing a spit bubble as she stared up at her. Then her little round face scrunched up. It didn't take long for Isabella to read the signs and understand what her daughter wanted.

This would be her first time breast-feeding, and Isabella couldn't stop the worrisome tingle in her stomach. During her pregnancy, she'd read everything on the subject and had talked to several nursing mothers. She'd always felt informed and ready. But now, as she opened her robe and guided her child to her breast, she hoped their advice had stuck with her.

But she needn't have been apprehensive. Emily nuzzled as she found her way. At first, there was just a hint of pain, but it slowly subsided. And as her little girl suckled contentedly, finding her own special rhythm, Isabella believed this beautiful process was the most natural thing in the world.

And a moment she wished she could share.

She glanced up. Across the room, sleeping in the velvet chair by the fire, was her knight—minus the shining armor. It seemed that while she and Emily had been resting, Michael had taken off his shirt and hadn't put on a clean one. Not that she minded in the least.

As Emily took her first meal, Isabella let her gaze travel over him. His jet-black hair was mussed from work and sleep, his rugged features were relaxed, and his square jaw was dark with stubble. Her pulse jumped as her gaze moved downward to his chest. He was powerfully built with wide shoulders, a trim waist and a V of dark hair that disappeared beneath the waistband of his jeans.

Her hands itched to touch, her heart longed for him to be closer, but her mind kept those yearnings in check.

He lay there, sound asleep, his breathing as even as her child's. Lord, he certainly deserved the rest. He'd worked hard. He'd kept his promise and brought them both through the night safely. She'd never forget how he'd looked when he'd handed Emily to her.

Proud.

And so handsome.

And in the moment, in that moment when life had felt perfect, she'd wished that he was Emily's father and her husband. But she'd shooed the thought away as quickly as it had come. Michael was just a friend, and she needed to remember that while they endured these forced living conditions. He was a *friend,* and the man who had just paid a debt he'd never truly owed to her in the first place.

On a soft sigh, she forced her gaze away from her sleeping gladiator and put all her focus back on her daughter.

But in that velvet chair, the gladiator was far from asleep.

His eyes closed, Michael listened. It seemed that with every move, every sound Bella and Emily made, a deeper and more profound sense of protectiveness and closeness filled him. The feeling was completely foreign and not necessarily welcome, but he couldn't help acknowledging it.

When he'd first heard the sound of Emily suckling at her mother's breast, he'd been in turmoil. Questions had raced through his mind. Should he leave the room or stay? What right did he have to invade this private world? But his need to be close to them had superceded any sense of inappropriateness.

Just then, the ache in his thigh deepened and he had to move. As quietly as he could, he shifted forward in the chair and stretched out his leg.

"Michael?"

Her call had him cursing softly. The last thing he wanted at that moment was to disturb the peaceful mood that had settled over the room. But he couldn't ignore her.

He turned to look at her. "Yes?"

"I thought you were sleeping."

"My leg's a little cramped."

"Well, as long as you're awake—" she patted the empty space beside her "—I wouldn't mind some company."

His gut twisted. He was safe over here, safe to be part of the scenery and nothing more.

"You can stretch out your leg," she continued.

"Are you sure?" he said, hearing the slight edge in his voice.

"Yes, of course."

All thoughts of impropriety floated up the chimney

like smoke from the fire. Whether it was wise or not, he wanted to be close to them tonight, wanted to share what she was so willing to give. This storm had made it possible for him to forget his past and his anger for a little while. It had thrust all of them into some kind of dreamworld. And who was he to break the spell? After all, it'd break on its own soon enough without any help from him. In a couple of days Bella would leave with Emily, and he'd resume his normal way of life.

His jaw tight at that thought, he walked over to the bed and sat down beside her. Emily was snuggled against Bella's breast, content in her meal.

Isabella smiled up at him. "You must be exhausted."

He shook his head. "I'm fine. What about you?"

"I feel wonderful. Tired, but wonderful." Her gaze drifted to the window. "The storm seems to be lingering." She turned back to him. "Looks like you're stuck with us for a little while longer."

"And it looks like you're stuck with my cooking for a little while longer."

She laughed and glanced down at Emily. "Well, one of us, anyway."

Without thinking, Michael followed her line of vision. Emily's eyes were closed as she suckled. Bella looked so natural, so beautiful with her breast bared and a soft smile on her lips. It was the sweetest sight he'd ever seen. The sweetest and the—

He stood up and drove a hand through his hair.

Hell, no. He'd be damned before he'd put a name to that feeling.

Was he going crazy? Had this snowstorm brought dementia, as well as ghosts from his past? He needed to get out of this room for a while, away from this intimacy that drew him like a bear to honey.

"Why don't I go make you something?" he offered. "You must be hungry."

"I know I should be starving. I just had a few bites of sandwich last night before Emily came knocking. But I'm really not."

"You need to keep up your strength. The storm and the baby—that's a lot in two days."

Her eyes softened, and she gave him a small smile. "Don't go."

It felt like steel beams were being pressed against his chest. There was nothing he wanted more than to be with her at that moment. And that made him nervous.

Over the years he'd been no monk. Whenever he traveled, women were near. They knew who he was, they were wary of his reputation, but the fact that he was a millionaire several times over usually turned caution into curiosity.

Although he remained aloof, he respected women and was always up front with them, letting them know he didn't have serious relationships. The women who came to his bed had been all right with that arrangement, and after a night or two of pleasure they would part on good terms.

Above all, he avoided needing anyone or being

needed. And he could see that need, that emotional tractor beam, in Bella's eyes right now. Hell, he felt it himself, and it made him even more determined to put some distance between them.

"I'm going to make you another sandwich," he insisted with a trace of a growl.

Regret lit her eyes, but it quickly passed and she nodded. "All right. But after that I want you to get some sleep."

He nodded and left the room. The ache in his thigh traveled like a brushfire down his leg as he walked through the hallway. But his thoughts burned even more.

She wanted him to get some sleep.

He shook his head as he entered the kitchen and uttered the word "lights." If he slept at all, he was going to be doing it in that chair by the fire in her room. Because even though his mind warned him to stay as far away from her as possible, his sense of duty won out. As long as she and Emily were in his house, they were his responsibility.

But how could he explain that to her? he wondered as he put a mug of water into the microwave and muttered, "Boil." And how could he explain to himself the depth of protectiveness that raged inside him?

How was he going to get rid of it before it swallowed him whole?

Later that day Isabella woke from another nap to feed and change Emily's towel-diaper. She was just about to go into the bathroom and wash up when

Michael walked into the room, pushing some kind of cart.

"What in the world is that?" Isabella asked.

He looked at her, his expression serious. "It's a bed for Emily."

Her mouth dropped open, but she quickly recovered. While she inspected the two-level cart, her heart softened. Michael had made this for her daughter. This sexy, bristly man had made a cradle for her baby.

After bringing her a sandwich a couple of hours ago, he'd told her that he had some work to do. With his reclusive ways, she really hadn't expected to see him again until evening. But he'd surprised her.

Something he'd been doing a lot of over the past few days.

"How did you do this?" she asked, switching a fussy Emily to her other arm.

"I unscrewed the top shelf of a computer cart and secured one of my housekeeper's wicker laundry baskets in its place. Then I reworked a feather pillow to make a soft lining and covered the whole thing in a clean sheet." He glanced up at her. "Do you think it'll be all right?"

Isabella couldn't help but smile. Did she think it would be all right? It was amazing. The contraption looked sturdy and safe. A perfect place to change Emily, and a perfect bed for her, too. And with wheels on all four corners, the cart was mobile. "It's just wonderful. Thank you."

He nodded. "I also cut up some more towels for

diapers.'' He gestured to the lower shelf neatly stacked with makeshift diapers.

She shook her head. ''You've thought of everything.''

He shrugged nonchalantly. ''Just trying to take good care of my guests.''

''You've given us the best of care, Michael.''

Michael stared at her, his gaze flickering from her eyes to her mouth, then back again. ''I'm going to make some dinner.'' Her eyes went a soft gray. ''No sandwiches tonight. I think you deserve to have a real dinner.''

His thoughtfulness only made her longing intensify. ''Would it be too much to ask you to take Emily?''

''Take her?'' Wariness filled his tone.

''I'd love to have a hot shower.''

''I don't know anything about babies, Bella. I—''

''You'll be fine.'' She gave him a reassuring smile. ''You're the one who helped bring Emily into the world. I trust you.''

He plunged a hand through his hair and walked over to the bed. ''All right. But if she can't stand me, I'm coming to get you. In the shower or out.''

Her breath caught as a ripple of wonder moved through her. Neither one spoke for a moment, and she wondered if he was going to take his promise back or at least clarify it. But he didn't. ''Dinner should be ready in a half hour.''

Her tongue darted out to moisten her bottom lip. ''Okay.''

Michael's gaze followed the movement, then he exhaled heavily and leaned down. "I'll see you in a half hour," he said as he backed up with Emily in his arms.

She felt heat blast into her cheeks. What was wrong with her? she wondered as she watched Michael gently place Emily in the basket, then wheel her out the door. Acting like a silly schoolgirl, instead of a new mother.

On a dejected sigh, she pulled back the comforter and headed for the bathroom. Her adolescent crush was blossoming into full-fledged hankering, and if she didn't get out of this house soon, she'd be in serious danger of that hankering growing into something stronger.

Something that wouldn't diminish in a few days like the early winter storm that raged outside.

Isabella remained under the hot spray for a good twenty minutes, loosening up her stiff and sore muscles before lathering and shampooing her way to squeaky clean.

After blow-drying her hair and changing into a pair of sweats that Michael had given her, she left the room feeling refreshed, but missing Emily terribly. How strange that in less than a day she couldn't envision her life without Emily, she thought as she walked down the glass hallway.

Opera music played and the scent of baked chicken spilled through the rooms she passed, growing in pungency as she approached the kitchen. Her stomach rumbled as she paused in the doorway, her gaze fixed on the scene in front of her.

On the stove, green beans simmered in a pan and steam rose off what appeared to be a chicken casserole. But the real show was happening on the tile floor. A handsome six-foot-four giant in a red apron stood next to the center island cradling a soft, cooing baby in his arms, arms threaded with muscle beneath the black T-shirt he wore.

As he swayed to the music with Emily blinking up at him and blowing spit bubbles, Isabella's heart dipped. They looked so right together, so content, and she ached to join them. But this was no family moment, and she wouldn't pretend it was. She had more than her own heart to consider now.

"Arthur Murray?" she asked lightly as she walked toward them. "Twenty lessons?"

He stopped moving immediately, his expression and manner going from relaxed to tense in two seconds flat. "She was crying. It seemed to help." He raised a brow at her. "And I didn't want to interrupt your shower."

Isabella nodded. "Thanks." *I think.*

He placed Emily in Isabella's arms and walked over to the stove, his limp even more obvious than yesterday. His leg was obviously bothering him and yet he'd just been dancing to soothe her child. Isabella fought the longing that surged through her at that realization, along with the urge to ask if he wanted to sit and rest while she did the cooking. But as their relationship was a little tenuous, she didn't want to risk offending him.

Instead, she took a seat at the kitchen table and inhaled deeply. "Smells wonderful."

"Thank God my housekeeper packed a few of these away in the freezer," he said, pointing to the casserole. "This one's called roast chicken surprise."

"My favorite."

He glanced over his shoulder. "I thought chicken soup with stars was your favorite."

She laughed. "It was—when I was thirteen."

"Ah. But now that you're all grown up, you've chosen a far more sophisticated entrée for your favorite?"

"Exactly."

Amusement glimmered in those steely eyes of his.

"You know, you look like one of those cooking show chefs in that apron," she said as she placed Emily in her new cradle.

"And you look..." He paused and she glanced up to see his gaze traveling over her. "Well, you look damn good in my sweats."

Her gaze fell, heat flooding her cheeks. "Thanks, but I know what I must look like."

"And what's that?"

"Tired and...well, like I just had a baby."

"Listen to me, Bella." His tone forced her eyes to meet his. "I don't think I've ever seen a woman more beautiful."

She stared at him for a moment. And then she began to chuckle. She couldn't help it. "That's so not true."

"I can think of a few surefire ways to convince you."

Michael felt all the lightheartedness that had filled him just a moment ago fall away as if he'd been caught laughing at a funeral. Bella stared at him again, heat filling her sexy blue eyes. Was she going to ask him what those ways were? And if she did, would he tell her the truth?

Behind her, Emily started to fuss, breaking the mood. Bella turned to her daughter and Michael went back to fixing dinner.

"What's this she's wearing for a diaper?" Bella asked after a few moments.

Michael didn't turn around. "It's a T-shirt. I changed her. The towels are too bulky."

"What does it say on it?"

"'Computer Programmers Know How to Use Their Hardware,'" he said dryly. "My housekeeper gives me a different one every Christmas. I'm sure she has another one all picked out for this year. She thinks they're very funny. Personally, I think it's funny that she actually believes I'm going to wear them."

"So you've made them into diapers?"

"Yes."

She laughed. "Sounds reasonable."

He set a plate of chicken and green beans in front of her.

"You're not eating with me?" she asked, taking a seat at the table.

"I don't—"

"I know, I remember—you don't eat with anyone." Her eyes grew thoughtful. "Someday I'm going to ask you why."

He sat down across from her and lifted a brow. "And maybe someday I'll tell you."

Bella ate slowly, but she ate all of it and he was glad. She needed food and rest, and he was going to make sure she got plenty of both.

At last she sat back and smiled. "You're a pretty good heater-up-er. I'm impressed. Two great feats in only thirty-one years. Dinner *and* diapering."

"Well, I have to confess that Emily helped me out with the latter. She's one patient girl."

Bella turned to her daughter and whispered, "That's what's called sweet talk, Emily. Watch out for boys who use it."

Michael smiled down at the little girl. "Don't listen to her, princess."

Bella raised a brow. "Princess?"

Where had that come from? And when was that snow going to stop? "She looks like a little princess with all that blond hair and those regal blue eyes, that's all."

And as he said it, he realized he could've been describing Bella. And she must've thought so, too, because she looked up at him with startled eyes.

He sat back in his chair. Endearments were coming from a mouth that rarely uttered anything but words involving business. And talking about nothing in particular, too—just banter? He'd always thought that banter was a waste of time. Get to the point, get the deal done, get out, that was his creed. At least, it had been until Bella had come here.

"So tell me about the pastry shop," he said, diverting his thoughts and the direction of the conversation to something safe. "When did pushing calories on your hometown become business, as well as pleasure?"

"About four and a half years ago. I'd been planning to open it in Fielding, but then I met Rick."

Emily fussed a little and Michael reached over, took the cart's handle and began to rock it back and forth. "And he didn't want you to work?"

She nodded, her gaze shifting from his hand on the cart back to him. "Rick really didn't want a wife who worked," she said. "But whenever I brought dessert to a social event or to a neighbor, they raved and raved."

"I bet they did." He rubbed a hand over his jaw. "I remember you making something pretty special for your dad and me every Sunday morning."

"What was that?"

"You don't remember?" He felt almost as disappointed as he was pretending to be.

She smiled softly. "I must be getting a little tired."

He stood up, concerned. "Of course you are. How about I walk you back to your room?" It was time for her to rest and time for him to say good-night, go upstairs and work, then wait for her to fall asleep and hope that tomorrow the sun would come out.

Emily was sleeping in her cradle on wheels by the time they reached the bedroom door. Bella turned to him and smiled. "I know I'm saying this a lot, but thanks. Thanks for taking such good care of us and being such a good friend."

He nodded even as that razor-sharp word plunged into his gut.

And to make matters worse, Bella stood on tiptoe and kissed him on the cheek. A soft peck, meant for a friend, but it reached him, deep down. And he couldn't be stopped.

His arm snaked around her waist and he pulled her close. Her eyes locked with his and he stared at her mouth like the hungry wolf he was.

"Are you going to kiss me?" she whispered, her breath warm and sweet.

"Would you stop me if I did?"

She shook her head. "No."

A growl escaped his throat as he bent his head and eased her into a series of soft kisses, gentle kisses. But she was no fragile flower. Pressing her tender breasts lightly against his chest, she parted her lips, urging him, welcoming him into her warmth. His pulse smacked against the base of his throat as he tasted, his tongue flicking, moving to a rhythm they created together.

Sweet as honey. He knew she'd taste like that.

"Michael," she breathed as she wrapped her arms around his neck and deepened the kiss.

Her saying his name seemed to drag him back from the brink. Somewhere in the cavern of his mind, he knew this was trouble. He knew he'd better back off before he welcomed that trouble with open arms.

With every ounce of determination he possessed, he dropped his ravenous grip on her waist and stepped back. "I'm sorry, Bella."

Her eyes glowed liquid blue. "I'm not."

Startled at her honesty, it took him a moment to recover. But he did. He had to. "That can't happen again. And I won't let it."

Her jaw quivered with frustration. "Why is that?"

"I don't want you getting involved with me."

"So you're protecting me from you, is that it?"

"In a sense."

Her jaw went tight. "I'm a grown-up, Michael. No longer thirteen and no longer in need of protection." She stared at him, trying to read his eyes. "That's it, isn't it? You don't see me as a woman."

Michael almost laughed at her suggestion. He wanted to tell her that he saw her as every inch a woman. He wanted to tell her he couldn't stop staring at her mouth, pink from his kiss. But what point was there in telling her either? She wasn't for him. She was going to be gone in a day or two and to say anything more or do anything more would be leading her down a pointless path.

"Good night, Bella," he muttered as he turned around and headed down the hall.

But it wasn't really good-night, he thought as he heard the bedroom door shut behind him. Not for him, anyway. As soon as she fell asleep, he'd be back at his seat by the fire, back to watching over his charges—and back to wanting more of what he'd just tasted, more than he would ever allow himself to have.

Five

Five days later the lines were still down and the snow still hadn't let up.

And neither had the impact of that good-night kiss on Isabella's mind and heart.

Even now as she stood at the stove making dough-nuts, she wondered what part of her mind had allowed her to start that madness—for she *had* started it. But how could she have known that her simple thank-you kiss would turn so heated?

Maybe because she'd wanted it to.

But look where her want had gotten her. A state of massive confusion.

She walked over to the makeshift cradle that held her sleeping daughter and kissed her softly on the cheek. Emily looked so content, curled up with her blanket in the basket that Michael had made for her.

Michael. She wished she could figure him out. Why had he pulled away from her? Was it Emily? Or was it that he couldn't let down his guard, move away from his past, forget about protecting her and see her as a woman? Had his compliments at dinner been just a ploy to boost her confidence?

The scent of dough turning swiftly into fragrant doughnut wafted through the air. As she plucked the sweet rolls from the hot oil and placed them on a paper towel, she was reminded again of the heat that lay just below the surface of that kiss she and Michael had shared.

He must feel something for her. After all, he still slept in her room every night. He crept in around 1:00 a.m., planted himself in that chair and pretended to be asleep as she fed her child. And every morning when she awoke he was gone.

He had pretty much avoided her during the day, except for the encyclopedia-inspired questions and suggestions about after-care for her and Emily. Concern, but with little emotion.

While time had moved slowly, she'd made use of the kitchen, cooking him meals and sending them up to him on the elevator. True, he'd always come to thank her, but then he'd disappear again. The only variation in that routine was when he offered to take Emily with him to give Isabella a break.

She appreciated his generosity with his time, but

couldn't help wishing that he would open up his heart, as well.

"You're going to draw the whole town up here on snowmobiles with that smell."

She turned at the gruff baritone and her breath caught in her throat. He looked so handsome, freshly shaven, hair wet from the shower, dressed in easy, modern black. So he'd finally emerged, she mused. They always seemed to have an enjoyable time together when he let his guard down. Perhaps that was why he tried to avoid her.

As he paused by Emily's cradle and smiled down at the infant, Isabella wondered if she was given the opportunity, would she be able to help to heal the deep, hidden wounds and complicated past of this man?

"Draw the whole town, huh?" Isabella said, turning around and returning to her task. "Wow, that's the power of a simple doughnut."

She heard him walk toward her, felt him behind her. "They look far from simple, Bella."

As he stood behind her, peering over her shoulder, she couldn't stop herself from breathing him in. Spicy, woodsy and pure male.

She dunked a hot doughnut in the chocolate sauce she'd made. "I'm trying them out as a new recipe for the bakery," she said, even though this was no new recipe at all. In fact, it was that special treat Michael had given her a hard time about not remembering the night they'd…

Well, anyway, she'd never forgotten. She'd made

them so often she knew the recipe backward and forward. And every time she had, she'd thought of him.

"You know," she began, "I'd love an opinion on these."

"Looking for a taste tester?"

She shivered as his warm breath swept over her neck. "Something like that." She glanced over her shoulder. "If you can spare some time."

His gaze darkened. "I think I have a few minutes."

Why did he have to look so sexy? And why couldn't she stop being affected by him?

"Why don't you go sit down at the table?" she said quickly.

He hesitated, his eyes softening. "You've been cooking for me for days. You must be tired. I really should be making breakfast for you."

She shook her head. "Never thought I'd say it, but I don't really like being waited on." Besides, she liked cooking for him, but she wasn't about to reveal that little truth. Doughnuts bubbled in the oil and she went back to work, calling over her shoulder, "Take a seat and I'll bring them to you."

"You made coffee, too." He sounded pleased.

She waved a hand at him. "It was simple. I just said, 'Coffee.' I'm really getting the hang of everything around here." Just in time to leave, she thought as she put a few warm chocolate-dipped doughnuts on a plate and brought them to him.

He glanced up. "You're not having any?"

She cocked her head to the side and grinned. "I don't like to eat with anyone."

Amusement lit his eyes. "That's *my* line."

"Nope. Your line is 'This is one *good* doughnut,'" she said, returning to the stove.

Out of respect, she kept her back to him as he ate. At last he sighed and said, "Nope. Not good."

She whirled around, her heart on the floor. "What do you mean? What's wrong with them?"

"They're not good, Bella." He leaned back in his chair. "They're great. Even better than I remember."

She tossed a dish towel at him. "You jerk."

He caught the towel and grinned. "Gotcha."

This gruff, teasing side of him was new and as potentially addictive as the chocolate that lingered on the side of his mouth. Impulsively she walked over to him and extended a hand toward his face. "You've got—"

"What?"

"A little chocolate…" She touched the side of his mouth just as his hand clamped over her fingers.

They stayed like that for a moment, their eyes locked, heat passing from his fingers to hers. She needed to let go, look anywhere but in those wolf eyes that pinned her where she stood.

She glanced up, then sucked in a breath. "The snow's stopped."

He released her and turned around. "What?"

"The snow. It's stopped."

For the next fifteen minutes, they remained in the kitchen, silent as two sentries, watching the gray bales of cotton in the sky part and allow the early November sun, insistent on being seen, to needle through.

Michael's words broke both the silence and the five-day illusion of domesticity. "By noon tomorrow, the roads will be clear."

Isabella nodded, her throat tight. "And Emily and I will be going home."

He didn't answer. He just watched as a beam of sunlight slowly crawled its way across the kitchen tiles.

"The Wulf" paced, only partly aware of the pain shooting down his thigh as he stalked across the hardwood floors of his den the following day.

The roads had been cleared and Bella had left closer to two in the afternoon, but Michael wasn't going to quibble about being off by a couple of hours. It was enough that she and Emily were gone.

Debt—paid in full.

He shoved a hand through his hair. He should've felt relieved to be rid of them. After all, they'd interrupted his life and his solitude. But relieved wasn't what he felt when, just an hour ago, Thomas Pinta had come to the house. The doctor had examined Bella and Emily thoroughly, deemed them healthy, then took them back into town with him to their new home.

No, not relieved. *Concerned* was more like it.

Michael tossed a sheet of paper onto his desk. He was up to his ears in the remote relay voice-command system that he'd already sold on his recent trip to L.A. That was where his mind should have been. On the groundbreaking software that was going to make him a lot of money. Or on the real reason he'd gotten into this racket in the first place: to help people live easier, safer lives.

It was his biggest project to date. It was due in six weeks and it would be delivered in six weeks.

And he couldn't concentrate worth a damn.

He hadn't gotten that kiss out of his mind or the need to feel and taste her again from his soul. And tonight, when he went to that now empty room and sat in his chair by the fire, he knew he'd miss the closeness and the sweet sound of Bella breast-feeding Emily.

How could he expect to concentrate when he had no idea if Bella and her baby were safe? What if another storm came and she was still cleaning the place? What if the cleaning crew couldn't make it out of St. Cloud for a few more days? He'd never forgive himself if something happened and he wasn't there to help and protect them.

He stalked out of his office and into the elevator. Maybe he'd just run into town and check on them, bring Emily's crib and a set of his long-range communication devices. Then, if she needed him, she could reach him right away no matter what the weather.

That should ease his mind and allow him to get back to business, he thought as he grabbed his coat and headed to the garage.

At least they had heat, Isabella thought as she glanced around the dusty apartment. Getting this place together was going to take at least a week, and there was nowhere else for them to stay in the meantime—the hotel was full.

She hadn't thought her apartment would be this bad. Shoot, she hadn't thought about anything except getting away from the man who made her knees turn to jelly and her heart fill with longing. An impractical reason for bolting, but around Michael… So off she'd gone with Doc Pinta.

The kindly old man had taken her first to the cemetery to see her father, then to the general store to get diapers and other supplies for baby and home. With sympathy in his tone, the doctor had told her that he wished he could offer her and Emily a room at his home, but with no one to help her until the holidays, Mrs. Dalton was staying with him, recuperating from the fall on her hip.

Trying to appear confident, Isabella had thanked him for his thoughtfulness and let him know that she had calls in to a few of her old high-school friends.

But that was a lie. She hadn't called any of her friends. Not Connie the redhead Rickford or meddling Molly or pint-size Wendy. She just couldn't. Not yet. Not with the past so unexplained.

When she'd first moved to Chicago, her friends had tried to call her for months, but Rick had been adamant about cutting off all ties to the past. Back then, she hadn't cared that his behavior was controlling, she'd just wanted the marriage to work, so she'd told herself that he just wanted to start a new life with her. But that dream had quickly faded. After he'd died,

Isabella had wanted to call, wanted to write, but she'd been afraid that her friends wouldn't forgive her. So she'd decided to wait until she'd returned to Fielding to explain things.

Speaking to each of them in person was the right thing to do. But after being estranged for so long, the first round of communication couldn't be asking for a place to stay.

She needed to solve this mess on her own.

"This place looks likes a train wreck."

Isabella whirled around to see Michael standing in the doorway of her apartment, looking like a Wall Street executive in a long black wool coat, expensive leather boots peeking out from beneath the hem of black pants. The frown lines around his mouth deepened as he glanced around the place. Then Emily began to fuss, letting out little bleats of distress that caught his attention.

"Hello, princess," he said, walking into the room and automatically reaching for her.

Isabella's heart lurched. She hadn't expected to see him until the spring thaw—until she'd had time to stop missing him. But no matter what she felt, she couldn't halt the smile that broke out on her face. "So what're you doing down here in the flatlands?" It was strange, but with him around, the mountain of work didn't seem as much like Pike's Peak as it had a moment ago.

"Seeing if you needed any help," he said, expertly cradling a now serene Emily against one strong arm. "And it looks as though you do."

"We're doing just fine. We'll get this place together in no time."

He didn't dispute that, but merely said, "I hear the hotel is full because of the storm."

That piece of news sounded even worse the second time around. "That what you hear?"

He nodded.

Life and the weather had thrown her a curve ball. But over the past eight months she'd grown strong enough to catch it, and without a mitt if she had to. "I have the newspaper. I'm expecting to find a room for rent by the end of the day." She could hope, couldn't she?

His mouth was drawn into a thin line, his brow furrowed. "Didn't anyone ever teach you not to expect anything?"

She chuckled. "Is that dreadful moral support the only kind of help you're offering?"

"No. This is." With his free hand, he took a set of keys out of his coat pocket and tossed them to her.

"What's this?"

"That room you were looking for."

She glanced at the keys, then back up at him.

"You need a place to stay while you're getting this one together, right?" he asked as he looked down at Emily. The little girl's gaze was fixed on him.

"Right," Isabella said slowly, hating where this was going.

"So why don't you and Emily come back and stay with me until then?"

Reaching out, she eased her daughter from his

powerful arms. It was a protective instinct, she knew. Emily was only an infant, but Isabella didn't want her getting even the tiniest bit attached to Michael Wulf. She knew how it felt to lose him. "No, we couldn't."

"Why not? It's a comfortable place."

Too comfortable, she wanted to tell him. Just being near him again had her wishing for things that would never come.

He glanced at her with hooded eyes. "Staying with me a few more nights isn't that big of a deal, Bella."

Yeah, maybe not for a man whose heart is locked up tighter than an oyster shell, she thought. Michael's past had taught him well. Her past had only intensi-fied the yearning for the kind of life, and the kind of love, her parents had enjoyed.

But what was the alternative? She wasn't going to call her friends, and the hotel wasn't going to grow another room.

"I appreciate the offer, Michael. But why would you even want us there? You made it pretty clear that we were in the way."

His jaw bunched. "What are you talking about?"

"You hide away, bury yourself in work and hardly come out, unless it's to thank me for making a meal."

"Work is what I do," he said, his voice distant. "It's the most important thing."

"Is it?"

His eyes narrowed. "What are you trying to say?"

Isabella exhaled heavily. "It just seems to me like lately there's something else that's just as important to you as your work. And that's paying back what you perceive to be a debt.'' She looked up into those familiar dark eyes and said what had been on her mind almost every moment since their brief kiss. ''This debt is paid. You don't have to do anything more for us out of gratitude.''

He shrugged. ''I'm only doing what's right.''

Emily gave a soft little sneeze.

Michael frowned. ''And don't you think you should do what's best for Emily?''

Her chin lifted indignantly as she pulled the blanket more snugly over her little girl. ''I'll always do what's best for Emily.''

''Glad to hear it.'' He nodded as though her ire was exactly what he was aiming for. ''First thing tomorrow, I'll have my housekeeper come and help you get this place—''

''That's not necessary, I'm perfectly capable—''

''Her name is Sara, and she's the best.'' Barely stopping for breath he continued. ''I had your car towed to the shop, and you can borrow one of my SUVs until it's ready. And while you're cleaning and getting the store fixed up, I'll watch Emily. Except when she needs to be fed, of course.''

Her mouth dropped open. ''Michael, you have work to—''

''She's no trouble.''

Isabella was ready to refuse him again, but she stopped. Was the fight really worth it? Michael Wulf was being kind, being a friend. And she and Emily needed both right now. They were in a pickle Isabella hadn't planned for, and she couldn't allow her pride to override practicality.

She sighed. She knew what he was offering was the best thing for her daughter. And she would sacrifice anything to keep her baby safe and healthy. Even her heart.

He lifted a brow. "Deal?"

She nodded slowly. "Deal."

"My car's outside—with a car seat in it."

"Where did you get a car seat?"

"I stopped by Thomas's. He loaned me the one he had in his car. He said we could keep it for as long as we need it. His great-nephew's outgrown it now."

We? We could keep it? As long as *we* need it? The words made her knees as weak as butter, but she wasn't going to allow her body to misinterpret the message. No matter how badly her heart wanted to follow suit. She had to be absolutely clear about his intentions, or lack thereof, going in if she was ever going to survive.

"You were pretty sure I was going to say yes," she said finally.

"I knew your good sense would prevail."

"Well, you're hard to say no to, Michael."

He nodded. "As long as you understand that, then you won't object to my taking the two of you shopping for a few things you need."

Michael ambled up to the counter at Molly's Mother and Child and added three more of what Bella called "onesies" to his already growing pile of clothing, blankets, toys and other baby accessories that looked essential. He could feel Bella watching every move he made. With Emily asleep in her arms, she stood there, aghast, shaking her head first at the pile, then at him.

"I'm taking enough from you, Michael," she scolded for the fourth time in as many minutes as she unbuttoned the top button of her thick navy coat. "Staying at the house, borrowing the car, accepting help from your housekeeper. I won't accept this. *I'm* buying Emily what she needs."

"This—" he pointed to the pile of clothes "—isn't a whim, Bella. This is a birthday present."

Her pretty blue eyes narrowed. "Birthday present?"

He wasn't about to let her win. He had millions and no one to spend it on. And this was the first time he'd ever felt pleasure in buying something for someone.

"She's a week old today," he said simply.

Bella just stared at him, but he saw an ounce of surrender lingering behind that indomitable gaze. So he moved in swiftly. "It's rude to refuse a gift. You don't want to be rude, do you?"

"Of course I don't want to be rude, but—"

"Good, because for a moment there I was starting to feel a little wounded." He touched his chest, where his heart was rumored to be. "Like I wasn't good enough to give Emily a present."

At that she burst out laughing. "You could sell an egg to a chicken, couldn't you."

His brow rose as he plunked down a bunch of baby bottles next to the cash register. "Quite possibly."

"Are you finding everything okay, Isabella?"

Apple-faced Molly Homney scooted around the desk and gave Bella a wide smile, her gaze flicking warily to Michael. He was used to looks like that. He rarely came to town, and when he did he didn't even pretend to be friendly. Hell, half the kids that had teased him way back when had stayed in Fielding as adults—including Molly Homney—and he wasn't interested in making nice with people who only wanted to get to know him now because he could buy the entire town if he had a mind to.

But then again, this woman had been a friend of Bella's. So for her, he would be agreeable.

"I think we've found more than enough," Bella said on a laugh.

Molly sighed. "Did I say how good it is to see you again, Isabella?"

"Yes, you did. But I don't mind hearing it again."

"We missed you so much. The girls are going to be ecstatic when they see you and little Emily." Molly shook her head. "You're just so darn lucky. Since the day I opened this store, Herb and I have been trying and trying, but no baby yet."

"It'll happen," Bella assured her. "When you least expect it."

Molly leaned forward and whispered, "The fun's in the trying, right?"

Bella's gaze flickered toward Michael, then she

looked down at Emily and said softly, and not at all convincingly, "Right."

Michael knew that Molly hadn't missed that glance, and he also knew that the implications of it would be all over town by morning.

Most people already knew that he'd delivered her child. He wasn't looking to ruin her reputation. She'd just returned home, and the rumor of a romantic involvement with the Wulf was only going to hurt her standing in the community.

Michael pulled out a credit card. "Since you left your wallet at the shop, let me get this and you can repay me later."

Bella's eyes widened and her lips parted as though she was about to protest. Just then, Molly reached under the counter, and Michael took the opportunity to lean toward Bella and whisper in her ear, "Repay me in doughnuts. Every morning."

He heard her sharp intake of breath, and something inside him shifted. Damn, she smelled good, he thought, breathing in her delicious scent one more time before he straightened.

After Molly had rung everything up and bagged it, she turned to Bella. "Is your apartment ready yet, or do you need a place to stay?"

"I'm staying with a friend."

Bella answered the question with no reserve and no embarrassment. She'd also had an out, Michael mused, but hadn't taken it.

"Not Connie?" Molly asked.

"Nope."

"Or Wendy?"

"No."

Molly's gaze flickered toward Michael. He raised a brow at her. She quickly returned to her task of bagging up the merchandise.

Bella was smart enough to know that Molly knew exactly who that friend was, yet she'd spoken with pride in her voice. Only one thing had really changed in fifteen years. Bella was still strong and principled, but today when they'd parted, he wasn't willing to let her go. Not yet.

Molly smiled at Bella, then at Emily. "Call me and we'll get the gang together."

Bella thanked her old friend, then gathered up Emily and left. Michael followed them out of the store.

"Staying with a friend, huh?" he said as he opened the car door for her. "I think she knows exactly who you're staying with."

"I didn't lie." Bella placed Emily in the car seat, then stood and met his gaze. "I am staying with a friend. Right?"

Around them the wind picked up, swirling threads of snow into white tumbleweeds. Neither one of them seemed to notice. She was waiting for an answer to a simple question. But then again, nothing was simple between them as of late.

"Let's go home," he muttered, unaccountably irritated.

Her gaze remained on his for a moment, then she let him help her into the passenger side of the SUV.

What was the truth?

He didn't know. Jaw clenched, he put the shopping bags, changing table and crib in the back. He just didn't know.

Six

———

"**W**here should this go, hon?"

Abandoning her grimy bathtub for a moment, Isabella glanced up. Sara Rogers, Michael's housekeeper, held out a small unmarked box for inspection.

Isabella pulled off her latex gloves and reached for it. After a soft shake, a wave of comfort swept over her.

"Something special?" Sara asked.

"My mother's copper cookie cutters." A smile came to Isabella lips as she handed the box back to the Southern gentlewoman with her short gray bob, thin frame and big violet eyes.

"Oh, my. Well, then, we'll have to be real careful with this." Sara tilted her head and winked. "How about that large drawer off the fridge? I just wiped it down.''

''That'll be perfect,'' Isabella said, reaching for her work gloves. ''By the way, have I thanked you today?''

''Yes, you have, hon. Twice in fact.''

''Well, they say that the third time's the charm. So, thank you.''

Sara placed her hands on her hips and studied Isabella for a moment. ''Mr. Wulf's sure right about you.''

At the mention of Michael, Isabella's pulse quickened. ''Right about what? What did…Mr. Wulf say?''

A grin the size of Tennessee, her home state, broke out on Sara's face. ''That you're a good one.''

Isabella's eyes widened. ''What in the world does that mean?''

Sara laughed. ''Don't have a clue, hon, but in all the years I've worked for him, I've never heard him say anything like it.'' She winked again. ''I'm going to put this away and start cleaning that stove.''

After Sara was gone, Isabella went back to scrubbing the tub, but her mind remained on Michael and their living arrangements.

It had been a week since he'd invited her and Emily to stay with him, which she'd thought would be plenty of time to get her place in order. But she'd been wrong. Making the apartment livable and her father's old work space into a pastry shop was taking far more work than just surface cleaning and stocking shelves.

Sara was a godsend, but she was only there for a limited time every day. Old neighbors from town came for a few hours to help out here and there, but most of them wanted to use that time to catch up and find out about Michael's inventions and his intentions toward her. So she'd started politely refusing the offers, extending her guest pass at the ''glass house'' for a while longer.

But the reasons for the slow pace in finishing her apartment were more than her friends wanting to play catch-up or the amount of work to be done. The separation from Emily for more than a few hours at a time had been torture. Isabella had left bottles of breast milk in the refrigerator for Michael to give her, but she'd wanted to be there, too. So she'd started making excuses to come home and check on her, play with her and nurse her.

Michael never seemed surprised to see her turn up several times a day. In fact, he almost seemed pleased to have her there. But at night, he'd always revert back to the lone wolf that he was. Taking his meals alone, staying up in his office, working late. He still slept in that chair by the fire every night, however. She never asked him why. She didn't want her questions to run him out, to drive him back upstairs. He did enough of that. From dusk till dawn, she felt protected and cared for, and Lord help her, she counted on it.

The ring of the Fielding Elementary School bell

several blocks away interrupted her thoughts, and she checked her watch. It was noon. Connie and Molly would probably be arriving anytime now, ready to "help." Somehow the two of them had convinced Isabella that they were geared up to clean her living-room floor.

It felt good to be home now. As soon as Isabella had gotten the chance to explain to her friends what had happened over the past several years, she'd done it. And true to form, they had readily welcomed her back, even welcomed her into their homes if she had a mind to move from Michael's. But she didn't. With a "thanks, but no thanks" to her friends, she'd told them that she and Emily were content where they were and left it at that.

Sighing, Isabella rinsed out the tub, took off her gloves, tossed them into the trash, then left the bathroom to find the pair, mops in hand, standing in the middle of the living-room floor.

Connie gave her a smile. "Sara let us in."

"She's Michael Wulf's housekeeper, isn't she?" Molly asked, fiddling with a bottle of wood soap.

Isabella nodded. "Yes, she is."

Molly had never understood the concept of leaving any juicy subject alone. "We were just talking about the day he moved back here."

Connie rolled her eyes. "Not *we,* Molly. Just you."

Molly snorted. "Don't think I didn't see those ears of yours perk up when I mentioned that Alan Olson said when he delivered that grand piano up there last year, he saw an elevator in Michael Wulf's house."

When she turned to look at Isabella, Connie's brown eyes clearly telegraphed that what Molly said was true. "What *is* his place like, Isabella?"

Molly snorted. "Forget his place, what's *he* like?"

They both stared, waiting for her to give them a confirmation to all those "Wulf" headlines. "He's intelligent and serious and very patient."

Molly grimaced, obviously not hearing what she wanted to hear. "Well, he's certainly gotten handsome over the years. I noticed that right off the day you two came into my shop. But his attitude's the same."

Isabella bristled. "What are you talking about?"

"He didn't want to fit in then and he sure doesn't want to fit in now."

"That's not fair, Molly," Connie argued.

Molly shrugged. "I call 'em like I see 'em."

"He tried to fit in when he first came here," Isabella said, planting her fists on her hips. "And you all shut him out. Why should he be the one to bury a hatchet he never swung?"

Connie looked down at her dustpan. "I was one of those kids that picked on him. And when your aunt couldn't take him in and he had to leave Fielding, I felt so bad about how I'd acted. But honestly, Isabella, I don't think he would even listen to an apology now, much less accept one." Her gaze lifted and so did her brow. "He doesn't need us anyway. He's rich and successful and probably has a ton of fashionable friends in New York and Los Angeles."

"Well, he sure made friends with our little Isabella,'' Molly remarked, her lips curving into a Cheshire-cat grin. ''And Emily, too. He watches her during the day, doesn't he?''

Isabella lifted her chin. ''Yes, he does.''

''That's very generous of him.'' Connie smiled at her, and Isabella appreciated her for it.

''And who does he watch at night?'' Molly asked, her eyes sparkling.

Isabella's stomach clenched. Her friend's teasing was too close to home. ''His computer, I imagine.''

''Seriously, though, it really doesn't worry you at all?'' Molly asked. ''That…well, that someone like that is taking care of Emily?''

''Someone like what?'' Isabella demanded.

''You know, strange and a little frightening.''

Anger shot through Isabella's veins. White-hot anger. As much as she'd wanted to believe that the children of Fielding had grown into mature adults, her friend had just proved otherwise. She wasn't a bad person, just so uninformed. ''Michael Wulf is an extraordinary man,'' she said, her tone ominous. ''He has changed the world with his technology. I feel honored that he considers me a friend, and there is no one I trust more with my daughter.''

Molly blanched, her gaze shooting to the floor. ''I'm sorry, Isabella. I didn't mean to offend you. You know me, I get started yapping and I can't stop.''

The fire in Isabella slowly abated. ''It's all right.''

''I should get back to the store,'' Molly said, checking her watch before scurrying out the door, a trifle shamefaced. "I'll try and come over tomorrow to finish up the floor. Bye, all."

Isabella shook her head at the floor that hadn't even been touched.

Connie laughed. "She can be a pain in the butt sometimes, but she's relatively harmless. Unless you happen to eat one of her brown-sugar cookies, of course."

Isabella laughed along with her. "Yeah, I remember." She regarded her friend. "You think I overreacted, don't you."

Connie shrugged. "Maybe just a touch. But I have to say, if I ever need someone to defend me, I'm coming to you." Lifting a brow, she added, "So, does Michael have any idea that you're falling in love with him?"

The sound of splashing met Michael at the open bedroom door. He'd come to get the legal pad he'd left by the fireplace last night, but the sound diverted his attention. Bella was in the tub. His groin stirred at the vision of her naked and doused in suds. Driving a hand through his hair, he hoped to force that thought out. For God's sake, she'd just had a child two weeks ago. He shouldn't be having erotic thoughts about her. He shouldn't be having thoughts about her at all.

But when he walked into the room and glanced through the open bathroom door, he was saved from himself. Her hair back in a loose ponytail, Bella was fully clothed and giving Emily a bath. Inside the tub, the baby girl was lying in the soft cradle tub he'd gotten, her tiny hands splashing her mother with the inch or so of water.

He tried to stay quiet as he moved closer and stood in the doorway. But she must've felt him there because she glanced over her shoulder and smiled. "Pull up a towel and grab some shampoo. I was just about to wash her hair."

For Michael, giving a baby a bath was far from a routine task. Ask him to write a zillion lines of code for a complex program and he'd come through with flying colors. But he knew he couldn't say no to either one of the Spencer females.

He knelt beside Bella, rolled up his sleeves and grabbed the no-tears baby shampoo.

She tossed him a sidelong glance. "So, are you looking to add shampooing to your long list of baby tasks?"

He poured some of the yellow liquid into his hands and worked it into a lather. "Am I that transparent?"

"No, actually. You're rather difficult to figure out sometimes."

"Well, that's just force of habit," he said, gently rubbing the shampoo into Emily's pale wisps of hair.

"Interesting. And I thought that prickly-pear demeanor was by choice."

Michael turned to look at her sly grin and playful eyes. For a second he took stock of where he was and what he was doing. Sitting next to the woman that made him feel things he didn't want to feel, bathing another man's child. And yet, there was nowhere he'd rather be. He glanced down at Emily. She blinked up at him, her hand lifted up toward him.

Like a magnet to steel, he reached for her and she wrapped her tiny fingers around his thumb. Something shot up his arm—an electric shock of warmth, a tenderness, an astonishing emotion he'd never felt before and didn't understand. The intensity of it bowled him over and he slowly eased his hand away. "I'm going to let your mother finish up here, princess." He stood. "I need to get back to work."

"Really, Michael?" Isabella's blue eyes searched his now shuttered ones. "Couldn't you just put work aside for a half hour and…well, I don't know, live a little?"

His lips twisted. She saw too much and it annoyed the hell out of him. "I'm living just fine, Bella. Take a look around."

"You know I'm not talking about money or what it can buy."

"I'll see you later," he said as he turned to leave.

"From the safety of your chair by the fire?" she countered.

He stopped at the door, but didn't turn back around.

"I'm going to feed Emily and put her to bed," Isabella said, her tone patient but firm. "Sara made a roast and mashed potatoes, and I made a chocolate torte. I'll be in the kitchen in about a half hour. Have dinner with me."

Another battle broke out inside Michael from a war that had begun the minute he'd opened the door to a car covered in snow and saw its occupant. And that woman was asking him to do something more intimate than she could possibly imagine. She was asking too much. "Enjoy your dinner, Bella."

"Enya, *Watermark,*" Isabella told the CD player as she lit the ten votive candles that decorated the kitchen table.

Although she hadn't intended it, the room looked magical, glistening in the candlelight. The table was set for two with beautiful Prussian-blue place mats, pristine china that had never been used, shining silver and winking crystal. She'd even placed a bowl of fragrant herbs from the hydroponic garden in the center. To anyone who wasn't aware of her true relationship with Michael, the scene appeared set for romance.

Connie's query, the one Isabella had left unanswered, flickered across her mind. Did Michael know that she was falling in love with him? Would he even care to know? She rolled her eyes. Of course he wouldn't. He could barely accept the emotional ramifications when Emily touched him. He seemed incapable of closeness. And Isabella was starting to wonder if that would ever change.

She trudged over to the stove. However uncertain the future, she was determined to have a nice dinner tonight, whether he chose to join her or not.

While she sliced the roast, Isabella listened to Emily's soft, rhythmic breathing on the baby monitor that she kept close to her at all times. Her daughter had gone to sleep with just two songs and a kiss tonight, leaving Isabella with an evening to herself.

A low growl sounded behind her. "You win this battle, Bella."

Or not.

"And the war, too?" Isabella smiled to herself. So he'd actually come. Even after their disagreement earlier, he'd come. She continued to slice the roast, not wanting him to see the look of satisfaction on her face.

"That remains to be seen."

"So where's my peace offering?"

She heard him pull out a chair, sit, then expel a weighty breath. "You wanted to know why I eat alone, right?"

Isabella turned around and faced him.

His voice held little emotion as he spoke. "Up until the age of fifteen, I had absolutely no control over anything. Who I lived with, how I lived or where. Being with a huge group of other pissed-off kids, you can barely breathe. There's no space, nothing to make your own. Then I started taking my food up to my room or out in the yard—no one bothered me. It became my time, the one thing I could claim."

Isabella was amazed. She couldn't believe he was telling her this. All she wanted to do was throw her arms around him and let him know how honored she felt, but she knew he would hate such a gesture. So with a platter of steaming beef in her hands, she walked over to the table and said casually, "And now?"

His gaze fairly burned a hole in her soul. "For some reason, I can breathe when I'm with you."

Her hand paused in the middle of scooping up some potatoes. What did he mean? Was he talking about feeling comfortable with her? Could he breathe around her because of their friendship? Or something altogether different?

With a shaky hand, she filled his plate with potatoes and roast and green beans, then his wineglass with the same sparkling cider that twinkled from her glass.

"Need anything else?" she asked.

He looked up, his gaze moving to her mouth. "What are you offering, Bella?"

The urge to lower herself into his lap, kiss him silly and say, "I'm offering this—take it or leave it," was incredibly tempting. But the fear that he might choose to leave it overpowered the impulse. So she turned away from that searing gaze and sat down across the table from him.

"I'm offering good conversation," she said finally, her breathing uneven. "And a wonderful meal."

His gaze remained on her, and she wondered if he was going to pursue the discussion. But he didn't. He picked at his potatoes and went off on a different direction. "How's the shop coming along?"

She felt thankful for the lighter mood. They both needed it right now. Especially Michael. This being his first meal à la companion and all.

"The shop's not really coming along," she said. "I'm still working on the apartment."

"Taking too many breaks?"

A half smile came to her lips. "Hey, I have to

check up on you and Emily. See if you guys are having too much fun without me.''

''If we were, you'd never catch us.''

''What?''

He adopted a serious visage. ''It's like this—while you're away, I have the entire Ringling Brothers circus up here, then after they leave, Emily and I groove to some serious rock and roll.'' He raised a brow. ''Rolling Stones.''

She held her grin in check. ''And when I come home?''

He shrugged nonchalantly, then took a tentative bite of roast. ''We close up shop, and Emily goes straight to sleep.''

Feigning emotional injury, she sucked in a breath. ''No circus for me? No dancing to the Stones?''

''I'm sorry.'' His dark gaze moved over her, seeping into her pores like melting chocolate. ''You just can't get no satisfaction, sweetheart.''

Her short stint at lightheartedness suddenly dropped away. Heat rushed through her body and her mouth went dry as cotton. How could he disarm her in two seconds flat? It wasn't fair, especially when he was just playing and her heart didn't understand the rules of the game.

And in that instant, his decision about not eating with her seemed like a good one, a safe one, a smart one. Perhaps he could breathe well around her, but the air in her lungs always seemed to get caught when she looked at him.

One thing looked glaringly obvious: if she wanted

to leave this house with her heart intact, she was going to have to pick up the pace on getting her apartment ready.

But the problem was she didn't want to leave this house. Or him.

"I heard you defended me today," he said, dragging her back to the candlelit, Enya-playing present.

She cleared her throat. "I haven't the vaguest idea what you're talking about."

"Oh, you don't, huh?"

Darn that eavesdropping Sara and her Southern charm.

"So there was no discussion about how much I've changed? Or how little?"

Isabella took a sip of her sparkling cider to stall for time.

"How I've gotten stranger and weirder over the years?"

She fairly choked on her cider. "No one said weird. They…"

"What did they say?"

Putting down her knife and fork, she exhaled. "You know what it is, Michael? They don't know you, that's all."

"They don't need to know me." The amusement left his eyes. And just like that, she'd lost him again.

"Maybe they do. And maybe you need to get to know them."

He frowned. "Why the hell would I want to do that?"

"To put the past where it belongs," she argued.

"Or start to, anyway." She leaned forward. "They were stupid, ignorant kids."

"And what are they now?"

"Just townsfolk. Flawed like any others, but not out to get you."

He chuckled bitterly.

"Doesn't it get lonely up here?" Isabella asked.

"Not with you and Emily around."

"We're not going to be around forever." The words were out of her mouth fast, and their meaning settled over the table.

Anguished cries came over the baby monitor, saving them from further discussion. Isabella was on her feet and halfway to the door when she said, "I'm going to check on Emily."

"And I'll clean up in here," he muttered.

As she headed for her bedroom—his bedroom— Isabella pushed away the fierce determination that rose up and claimed her every time he was near. The determination that made her want to heal the man she was falling in love with before he dug himself into an even deeper hole.

But Michael Wulf didn't want to be saved, she thought as she entered the bedroom. Even with the tiny step he'd taken tonight, he was stubborn on every other subject relating to change. And she knew that the more she tried, the harder it would be for her heart to heal when she left.

Emily just needed a clean diaper and a meal. So after changing her, Isabella slipped into her nightgown, lay down on the bed and held her sweet little girl in her arms. Her daughter was happily suckling when Michael knocked on the door.

"Come in," she called softly.

He took one look at her and Emily and turned away. "I'll come back later."

"No." She swallowed hard. Heartache be damned, she wanted him close. She always wanted him close. For as long as it was possible. "Why don't you build a fire and stay?"

Michael stood there for a moment, his jaw tight as he decided what to do and what he wanted. After a few seconds he walked into the room, crossed to the fireplace and set some logs in the grate. It took only a moment for the tinder to catch and a fire to blaze. Then he sat down and stretched out his leg.

"You're early tonight," she said gently. "You usually don't spill in until after midnight."

"I know" was all he said.

The fire crackled, Emily nursed, and after several bouts of *Should I or shouldn't I?* Isabella decided to take a chance and ask for something she'd wanted since the night she'd given birth to Emily.

"Michael?"

"Hmm?"

Her pulse jumped around like a rubber ball. "Why don't you take that rebellion of sharing dinner with me one step further?"

He glanced over at her, so incredibly, rustically handsome in the firelight. "How would I do that?"

She would be gone soon, and so would these

strange and very wonderful moments of time. "Sleep with me."

His eyes went black as coal.

She scurried to clarify. "In the bed. We can share it. You insist on being in the room and...and I insist that you let that leg rest." She bit her lip.

He turned back toward the fire, and she wanted to die of embarrassment. What was she thinking? Why didn't she just get in the car, drive into town and moon the crowd over at Teddie's Pub and Pool? It would've been less humiliating.

After clicking off the bedside lamp, she exhaled and settled back further into the pillows. "Good night, Michael."

No answer came, not any verbal one, that is, but after a moment or two, he stood up and walked over to the bed. She held her breath, her heart pummeling her ribs as he lay down beside her, outside the covers and fully dressed. But she felt his warmth through the barriers.

"Night, Bella," he whispered as he put his arm around her.

As Emily continued to nurse, Michael moved closer, shutting off the small gap between them, and Isabella let her head fall against his shoulder with the understanding that this small glimpse of ecstasy would never be enough.

Seven

———

The afternoon sun submerged the room in clean yellow light. Michael stared at the computer screen, his fingers poised above the keyboard.

Nothing.

This was unheard of. His mind was normally spilling over with project ideas. But this one in particular had him stumped.

He heard Emily's cry erupt from the baby monitor beside his mouse pad. Because he watched her during the day, he kept it close to him. The little girl now sounded very distressed, he thought, staring at the device. After a moment, Bella's soft soothing voice came over the monitor.

Michael pushed back his chair, wanting to go to them. Then he stopped and shoved himself toward the desk. Dammit, he couldn't react this way every time Emily cried and Bella went to her. Two weeks of sleeping in the same bed, eating dinner together, they were starting to fall into a routine. A very unwise routine.

No matter how right it felt each night stealing into bed with her, no matter how strong the urge to taste her again, pull her closer, feel the softness of her against him, he wasn't a part of their family. Sweet little Emily lay between them as she nursed reminding him, warning him to remember who they were to him. Two individuals he'd sworn to protect.

And that meant protecting them from himself, too.

Bella had told him that her apartment and the bakery were almost ready. Soon they'd be gone. That thought pierced his chest. But even with the frequency in which he had to remind himself of their departure, the blade of pain to come thankfully hadn't reached his heart.

The soft whirr of the elevator rising tore his thoughts away. Bella was always coming upstairs without an invitation. In spite of himself, he looked forward to her impromptu visits, although he could never tell her that.

But when the metal doors parted, it was no curvy blonde with liquid-blue eyes that emerged.

"Hello, Michael."

"What the devil are you doing up here, Thomas?"

"This your office?" Doc Pinta's gaze worked the room like a mother-in-law looking for dust.

"Yes, it is," Michael answered dryly. "How did you get up here?"

"Isabella."

Michael snorted. "Of course. As if I really needed to ask. That woman has invaded my life." And damn if he didn't enjoy it. No one needed to know that sad fact, however.

Thomas fell into a leather chair, crossed one booted foot over his knee and grinned. "You could always tell her to go."

"Their apartment isn't ready yet."

"And are you going to be ready to let them go when it is?"

"Of course I am," he said a little too forcefully. "This, the two of them staying here, well, it's been just a…" He paused.

Thomas's brow shot up. "A what? A good deed?"

"Something like that."

The older man nodded, amusement flashing in his eyes. "So what are you doing for Thanksgiving?"

"The same thing I do every year."

"Hole up in your house?"

"Work."

Thomas chuckled. "Ah, yes, of course."

"Normally I'd stay at the computer from dawn to midnight, but—"

"This year you might stop at dusk?"

"I was going to say that I'll probably stop for an hour or two. Maybe have something with Bella and—"

"Isabella and Emily are coming to my house."

Michael paused. "Are they?" He let that bit of information wash over him like ice water. He felt like three kinds of fool for assuming Bella was staying here with him tomorrow. But what could he do? As his latest mantra warned, they were guests—and soon-to-be-departing guests. Her life and where she chose to spend it and whom she chose to spend it with had nothing to do him.

"And I'm going to put it out there again this year," Thomas was saying. "If you can tear yourself away from the office for an evening, we'd love to have you, too. It won't be anything fancy. Just family."

Even though he and Thomas had always been on friendly terms, Michael had never crossed that line with him. No matter how many times the doctor and his wife invited Michael to their home, he wasn't about to get involved in some warm and fuzzy family thing.

Michael shook his head. "I don't think so. But thanks for the invitation."

"Well, if you change your mind…"

"I won't."

Thomas nodded, then turned and walked into the elevator. "I sure do love Thanksgiving. Reminds a person of all there is to be thankful for in this life, don't you think?"

The door closed on Thomas's query, and for moment Michael stared at the door that had shut him off from everything human until Bella had traipsed back into his life.

A low growl escaped his throat as he turned back

to his work. This, *work*—that's what he was thankful for. He didn't need a holiday to bring on that bit of self-awareness.

"You have to peel them, Michael." Isabella laughed as she dipped into a kitchen drawer and came out with an apple peeler. It was strange, but she knew the workings of Michael's kitchen better than he did. The intimacy of it all still surprised her.

Michael grumbled as he stripped the apple of its protection. "I don't know why I'm helping with a dessert I'm not even going to eat."

"Neither do I," she replied cheerfully. "Why don't you go back upstairs and work?"

"I'm working out an idea in my head." He kept peeling. "I needed some air."

It was how they were. One grumpy and one excessively merry. They seemed to balance each other out, Isabella thought. During the day they each worked, while sharing chores and sharing Emily. At night Michael read Emily a story until she fell asleep and Isabella made dinner. Then, when it was time to go to bed, they lay together while Emily had her late-night snack. They tried not touch, but inevitably each night they'd lose that battle and by morning they would be cuddled together with Emily between them.

Isabella rolled out the pie crust with a fervor that erupted inside her whenever she thought about Michael in her bed. But although she couldn't smother the heated workings inside, she tried to remain cool in demeanor on the outside and opted for idle conversation. "Why aren't you going to Thanksgiving dinner tonight? And don't tell me it's work."

"It *is* work."

"This is a holiday, Michael."

"I don't believe in holidays."

With steady hands, she placed the crust in the glass pie plate. "What do you mean you don't believe in holidays? You had Christmas with me and Dad."

"I have two weeks to deliver my software to Micronics." He started cutting up the apples. "I can't afford any more nights off."

He wasn't fooling anyone with that grouchy declaration. All those nights with Emily and dinners with her hadn't really cut into his work schedule at all.

"Maybe I can help you," she offered.

"Help me what?"

Oh, Lord. That was a loaded question. But one step at a time. "If I can help you solve this problem you're working on, will you go to the Pintas with me?"

His eyebrows rose a fraction.

"C'mon, give me a chance," she said. "I have some great ideas."

The skepticism shadowing his gaze was no surprise, but as she poured the apples into the waiting pie crust, he explained, "The software I've created is for a Web-to-home connection. My original proposal included the ability to turn the thermostat up and down over the Internet, arming or disarming the home-security system, watering the plants and the yard."

"That's sounds wonderful." Fragrant cinnamon

and nutmeg wafted through the air as Isabella sprinkled the spices and sugar over the apples, then dotted the whole thing with butter.

"I don't feel it's enough. I want to add a feature for parents that will allow them to spend more time with their children. Everyone's so busy, especially mothers. I thought that speeding up the small things like having the bathwater already drawn would leave more time for the actual bath."

"It would."

"But I need a few more ideas."

"Okay." Her mind worked as she rolled out the top crust. "I can certainly give you a mother's perspective. How about being able to use a Palm Pilot to start a bottle warming while Mom's still on the drive home? Or an automatic inventory system that keeps track of how many diapers and wipes are used and reorders through an online shopping list?" She turned to face him. "Or you could design a car-pool program where the mom who's driving can send instant messages to the other children's mothers letting them know their kids have safely arrived at their destination."

Michael didn't say anything for a moment, just stared at her, and Isabella wondered if her suggestions sounded ridiculous. But then he moved toward her, backing her against the counter, his hands bracketing her hips, and she couldn't think at all.

His hooded gaze level with hers, he whispered, "Has anyone ever told you how smart you are?"

Caught, pinned, trapped by the sexiest man she'd ever laid eyes on. "I've heard that once or twice."

His eyes moved to her mouth. "How about how beautiful you are?"

She swallowed, but her voice remained caught in her throat. She wanted to kiss him. Just one, then she could go back to town happy. Oh, who was she kidding? A kiss would never be enough. But it was a start.

Her silence seemed to make Michael draw back. "Sorry about that."

Dammit. "About what?" She fought to keep her voice light, playful. "Giving me a compliment?"

But Michael's eyes were shuttered, his mouth drawn into a firm line. "No. It just sounded like a come-on and…" He trailed off.

"And you would never come on to me, right?" she finished for him.

"Bella, listen, you deserve more than—"

She put a hand up. "I have a lot of work to finish, Michael." She had no interest in listening to his excuses for not touching her, no matter how noble and rational they sounded. After such a crummy marriage, she wanted the real thing. She wanted a man who wanted her and wasn't afraid to admit it.

"If you'll excuse me," she said tightly.

"Fine. I'll go." His eyes darkened. "But I'll see you later."

She watched him walk out of the kitchen, all too clear about what he meant. He'd see her in bed later. He'd lie beside her in the spirit of protectiveness, while her hormones raged and her body craved what it couldn't have.

She needed to leave, go to her own home. Because what had started as a fantasy was slowly becoming torture.

Michael stood on the Pintas' doorstep with a poinsettia and a bottle of that sparkling cider Bella liked so much. Sara had thoughtfully made him a small turkey with all the fixings before she'd left for her own family celebration, but he'd packed it up, put it in the fridge and left the house.

He told himself that he was here because he owed Bella. Those ideas she'd spouted off like tennis balls from an automatic feeder were pure genius and would no doubt make Micronics do backflips. But that nagging voice that resided too close to his heart relayed an altogether different story: he couldn't eat alone anymore. Or maybe it was that he couldn't eat without her. Either way, he was in trouble.

The door opened and Thomas presented him with a grand smile. "You came."

"Don't rub it in," Michael grumbled.

Thomas laughed as he escorted Michael inside. The scents of turkey and apples were heavy in the air. First stop was the kitchen where he presented Ruth with the poinsettia and shook the hand of her younger son, Kyle, who was sampling his mother's stuffing and mashed potatoes with a fork. Michael thanked them for inviting him and went into the living room.

Looking extraordinarily beautiful with her long

blond hair loose, a little makeup and that killer smile, Bella sat on the floral couch beside Thomas's oldest son, Derek, talking animatedly. The Pinta sons had been athletes in high school and had had no taste for teasing a young Michael as their schoolmates had. They were pretty decent guys...well, as much as Michael had gotten to know them in the four years he'd been back in Fielding.

Derek had been living in Minneapolis for a few years practicing law, and he looked the part. Casual but expensive suit, slicked-back hair and manicured hands. And, Michael noticed with a trace of annoyance, those hands were holding a crying Emily.

The threesome looked way too comfortable. He knew that someday Bella might have a new husband and Emily would have a father. But that day wasn't today. They still lived with him. And until they moved out, they belonged to him.

"This is a surprise," Bella said as both she and Derek stood up and walked over to greet him.

"We had a deal, right?" Michael said, glancing at her form-fitting blue skirt and blouse. One month and already her figure was all breath-catching curves. Where was the mercy?

She shrugged, her smile tentative. "I wasn't exactly sure."

Emily continued to cry, and Bella took her from Derek, but soon that cry turned into a wail.

"Let me take her," Michael said, easing the little girl into his arms.

Bella smiled at Derek. "He's something of a baby-whisperer."

A very content Emily remained in his arms all through dinner. From time to time, Bella would offer to take her. His excuse was always the same: Emily was fine where she was.

No one made a big deal out of Michael's surprising interest in joining a social event. The awkwardness he'd expected to feel never came. He hated to admit it, but they were a nice group of people, no apparent hidden agendas. Over turkey and dressing and corn pudding, they discussed current events and told jokes. But when dessert time came, so did Michael's waiting cynicism.

"Before anyone takes a bite of either of Bella's delicious pies," Thomas began, "we each have to say what we're thankful for." He glanced at Michael and gave him a one-word explanation, "Tradition."

"My health," Ruth exclaimed.

"I'm incredibly thankful for my daughter," Bella said with a soft smile.

"Mom's sage and onion stuffing," Thomas's younger son offered. "Just the best."

Thomas looked around the table. "For all of you being here."

"Class-action lawsuits," Derek said, deadpan.

Everyone broke out into laughter and Michael hoped to hell that they'd forgotten him. To help that plan along, he picked up his fork and focused on his slice of apple pie. But soon he felt all their eyes on him and he glanced up.

"Come now, son," Thomas said with a hearty chuckle. "Hurry up. I'm dying to take a bite of this pie."

In the past fifteen years, right answers had flowed from his lips more smoothly than Bella's hot caramel sauce. But these people looked at him as though they could spot brightly packaged bull a mile away. "If it's all right, I'd prefer to keep it to myself."

Silence met his answer, and he glanced over at Bella. She smiled and nodded her head. "I think that's fair. But next year we'll expect an answer."

The room settled into approving laughter and enthusiastic pie eating. Michael, however couldn't take his eyes off his beautiful, and highly addictive guardian angel. She'd done it again. Saved him from the torturous crowd. And right now, if she asked him again if that debt he owed her would ever be paid, he knew the only honest answer would be...

No.

After she'd fed Emily and put her to bed, Isabella grabbed the baby monitor and headed down the hallway to the elevator—the same direction Michael had taken when they'd arrived home a few hours ago. It had been plenty surprising to see him at the Pintas', but gratifying to watch him take another step into life.

It made what she had to tell him easier. Almost.

She heard the rock music before the elevator stopped and the doors parted. Garbed in just sweatpants, Michael was stretched out on a workout bench, pressing a metal bar with a tremendous amount of weight on it over his head.

"Need a spotter?" she asked, crossing to stand over him.

"No," he grunted. "That's not what I need."

Her skin warmed at his words and their obvious meaning. Her gaze moved over him as he brought the bar to his chin and back up again. Taut stomach, powerful arms roped with muscle. A fine sheen of sweat glistened on his skin under the lights. Longing surged into her blood. Yes, she understood that hunger, that need.

But she couldn't tell him that. So she did the only thing she could. She plunged headfirst into why she'd actually come up here. "Well, you're missing out, Wulf. It's my last night to spot you."

He brought the bar down and secured it to the rack before he said, "Your last night?"

The smile she gave him was bright. "Emily and I are going to move into town tomorrow."

"Your place is ready?" His voice had an edge.

"It's actually been ready for a few days, but…"

He stood up, wiped his face and chest with a towel. "But what?"

Isabella watched the white cotton with envious eyes as it moved over his chest. Never again would she be able to stare at him so openly. No. She'd have to pine and long in the privacy of her new place. There was no point in telling him that she'd stayed here longer than necessary because being with him was as addictive as chocolate. She had to give herself a chance at a real life, a real love.

"I think I'm going to go downstairs," she said swiftly. "Get ready for bed. I'm pretty tired."

"So am I, Bella. You know that? I'm real tired." His gaze demanded she not look away.

"Well, it's probably all the bench-pressing," she said, gesturing at the weights.

He shook his head. "No, that's not it."

"Tryptophan in the turkey can really mess with—"

"I'm tired of pretending that I don't want you," he said as he caught her arm and gently pulled her to him. "Bella…"

"What?" Her voice shook with want and need and anxiety. This was so unfair. She was weak with him, didn't he know that? Didn't he understand how easily he could hurt her?

His mouth was too close, his eyes were growing too dark. "Would you like to know what I'm thankful for?"

She held her breath as the heat from his sweating body surged into her chest and shot straight downward.

"I'm thankful for that strange October day when the snow turned into a blizzard." He leaned in and kissed her mouth softly. "And I'm thankful that it wouldn't stop." His eyes never left hers, but his fingers moved to her blouse, opening the buttons one at a time.

She shivered, her legs like jelly.

"I'm thankful you let me bring Emily into this world," he whispered, his tone husky.

Isabella's breathing turned into short rhythmic pants as her mind and all good sense fell away.

He eased off her shirt, let it fall to the floor. "I'm thankful that you came back to stay with me a second time."

Cool air warred with the heat blazing on her skin.

"And I'm so thankful," he said, "that you came up here tonight and didn't pull away from me."

Was he serious? "I would never pull away from you, Michael," she said. "Never."

His gaze held hers as he reached behind her. Two little clicks and her bra fell to the floor. "You've driven me insane, Bella."

"Finally." The words came out in a rush as she buried her hands in his hair and drew his mouth to her breast.

It was the sweetest feeling in the world. So far removed from what she'd imagined or dreamed of. His mouth was gentle as he suckled, flicking the hardened bud with his tongue. If he could just let himself go, allow himself to feel for longer than a moment—longer than a kiss—she'd know in her heart that he was taking one more step toward life. And toward her.

"Bella," he whispered, "tell me this is all right.

It was more than all right. It was everything.

Abandoning her aching breast, he looked up at her, eyes dark as the night sky but overflowing with stars of desire. Maybe this was fantasy, maybe she was crazy for falling into the arms of a man who could never love her. But at this moment she didn't care. "It's perfect, Michael."

His eyes flooded with heat as he unzipped her skirt and told the lights to dim.

Eight

Michael knew he'd gone mad with a desire and a yearning he didn't dare stop to examine. If he did, he'd remember how wrong this was. He was Bella's protector and her friend. But right now, friendship was the last thing on his mind. Pleasing her the way she deserved to be pleased was his one and only mission, and he'd suffer the consequences of this foolish decision later.

Bella's mouth called to him and he brushed his lips over hers until she opened. The lower half of him contracted, hard as steel as her hot, urgent tongue slid into his mouth. A moment ago he wouldn't have believed it possible, this level of need. So unfamiliar, so forbidding. But this was Bella. She'd shocked him with more than his staggering desire for her. Everything he'd experienced in the past month had been different with her near.

With an animal growl, he eased down her skirt, then her sheer stockings, grazing her supple hips with his hands, until she stood before him in just a mere wisp of pale-blue lace. A hint of a smile touched her lips, and her eyes were bright and filled with hunger. The look fisted around his heart.

A muscle tensing in his cheek, Michael turned away for a moment. No one had ever ripped a pathway to his soul the way she did.

"I've thought about this too many times." He could hear the frustration in his voice.

He glanced up to see disbelief warring with that killer need in her eyes. "You have?"

"Every night, all night. And then there are the days..."

"Tell me what you imagined," she whispered as she slowly slipped off her panties.

Every ounce of control he possessed snapped like a twig in a tornado. Another growl escaped his throat as he picked her up, walked over to his desk and thrust aside all the papers. In a chaotic wave, they floated in the air a second before fluttering to the floor. But Michael hardly noticed as he sat her down on the smooth surface of his desk.

Bella's mouth fell open in surprise at the bold move, but her eyes burned with a fever his body recognized.

"You wanted to know what I imagined, right?" he

asked as he dropped into the leather chair directly in front of her.

She nodded, and he noticed that her pulse pounded violently at the base of her throat.

His eyes locked on hers, he moved his chair forward until the arms hit the metal desk. "I thought about filling my hands with you," he said as he reached behind her and cupped her buttocks.

Her breath rushed out. "Then what?"

He slid her toward him. "I thought about you spreading your legs for me."

She licked her lips. Slowly, she eased her knees apart. "And then…?"

A grin split his face. "Watch." He dipped his head and tasted paradise.

Isabella sucked in a breath as she felt Michael's tongue graze the slick heat of her. Windows surrounded them, leaving their actions and reactions open to the world. Out this far, surely no one was going to see them, but the element of erotic risk added to her already heightened sense of need.

Never in her life had she trusted a man so completely. Never in her life had she given herself so fully. But this was Michael, the man she loved, making her breath catch, her nipples tighten and her core flood with aching heat.

The feeling was so foreign it frightened her at first, but when she looked down, watching him move so tenderly, the fear gave way to pleasure. The soft, ragged strokes, the teasing, the pressure. Her mind went blank, totally white.

Then suddenly, through the haze, she felt him ease a gentle finger inside her. She gasped, took him fully. And as he gave her short, little thrusts, something happened. A storm began building inside her, a storm that only Michael could intensify, that only Michael could quell.

Frantic moans erupted from her throat. She felt wild, like a starving lioness with its prey in sight. Her instincts took over and she pressed herself closer to him, letting her head fall back. More than anything, she wanted to give herself to him, all that she was. She wanted him to know that only he could make her feel this way, make her react like this. But she couldn't remember how to speak.

Michael worked his magic as her body quaked. She was a racehorse, frantic, enjoying the journey but desperate for the finish line. She forced her heavy head to lift, her eyes to open. Deep and low, she shuddered at the sight of him, his dark head buried between her thighs.

Lost, she gave in, allowing the ripples of orgasm to take over her body. Squalls of torment crashed into her, and she shuddered. Heat thrashed through her core over and over.

But as the waves lessened in size and power, Michael didn't draw away. As if he knew how sensitive she was, he went on, slowly, building the tension anew with his tongue. Her mind slow, but her body wakening again, she welcomed the building heat inside her—then raging heat that came faster this time. And when lightning hit and climax came once again, she cried out her pleasure, then collapsed back onto his desk.

She felt weightless, replete, as though she were floating down a river of feathers. Gradually she began to mentally paddle to shore, certain that her love for Michael would never wane. She was his.

As her breathing slowed and her body temperature fell, she eased her eyes open. Michael stood above her, tousled hair, his chest once again glistening with sweat and the front of his sweatpants bulging with arousal. Lord, she wanted to touch him, feel his weight on her, feel him inside her. She wanted to make him feel what she was feeling right now. Reaching out, she took his hand and tried to pull him to her.

But his expression stopped her, and she released him. The frown lines around his mouth plainly showed that he wouldn't allow himself the same pleasure he'd just given her. His eyes were like onyx, his body language warning trespassers to beware. Isabella's heart lurched. He'd closed himself off again.

Suddenly she felt very exposed. She looked down to see her clothes mocking her from the floor.

Michael turned to face the window. "I'm not sorry about what just happened. Now you can never say…"

Quickly as she could, she picked up her clothes and dressed, frustration ruling her heart. "Never say what?"

"That I don't want you. Or that I don't see you as a woman. Because, I do." Staring out the window, he exhaled heavily. "When it comes to you, I seem to have no self-control."

For a moment she wanted to believe that his admission was a compliment, but she knew better. She knew he was afraid to care about anyone and anything, and she knew why. She wanted to storm out of the room, let her own anger war with his, but her love wanted to offer him comfort. She walked to the window and put a hand on his shoulder. "Michael, I know that—"

"Maybe it's good that you're leaving tomorrow," he said. "There's nothing for you here."

She dropped her hand from his shoulder. "Maybe you haven't noticed, but I'm not asking for anything."

"You deserve to ask, Bella. You and Emily deserve a man who believes in love, trust and happily-ever-after." His hands were splayed on the glass above his head as he stared out into the night. "You see those pictures on my walls?"

Her gaze swung to the etchings she'd noticed the first time she'd come up to his office. "Yes, I see them."

"They're here to remind me that they're as close as I'm ever going to get to a fairy tale."

Isabella stared at his back, his bitter tone washing over her. She'd had enough. She was growing weary. "If that's what you believe, Michael, then I'm sure it'll come true."

Turning, she left him at the window. She loved him

almost to the point of pain, but she wasn't going to beg him to give up the past that held him hostage.

She stepped into the elevator and said, "Second floor." If he wanted her, wanted the real love she offered, he knew exactly where he could find her.

In the world of the living.

Same road, same car, same driver, same passenger. But no snowstorm.

Michael glanced out the window of the town car as they sped along, half expecting to see Bella's clunker on the side of the road. But this time she wasn't there. More than likely she was happily baking away in her newly opened shop, listening for Emily's cry on her baby monitor, catering to a town that adored cream puffs and apple fritters.

Two weeks had passed with the speed of an ice age. He'd tried to keep his mind off them, but with Thomas calling almost daily to tell him how well Bella and Emily were doing, he hadn't succeeded very well. Sure, he was glad to hear that they were all right, but the calls served as thorny reminders of how empty his house was now. How empty he was.

After a week of that agony, he'd packed up and gone to California early, hoping that work would once again be his saving grace.

But while he was working with Micronics, the CEO had insisted on showing him a few sights. Everywhere Michael had gone, from the ocean to Hollywood and Vine, his mind had remained on his two ladies. How he'd wished that Bella and Emily were there with him. He'd actually felt jealous of the people in a tiny snow-covered Minnesota town—jealous because they were now the lucky recipients of Bella's time and attention the way he had been for almost a month.

He leaned back against the leather seat and crossed his arms over his chest. What a fool. He missed her laugh and the way she battled with him over anything and everything. He even missed her coming up to his office and interrupting him ten times a day. And that image of her on his desk…

He hadn't been able to work there since that night.

But he'd get her off his mind soon enough—he had to. Just as soon as he stopped by to thank her for her part in sweetening his deal with Micronics. When he saw her again, maybe this…spell she'd cast over him would finally disappear.

He snorted at the absurdity of that thought as the driver pulled up to her bakery. The first thing Michael noticed when he stepped out of the car was a shopkeeper's back-at-such-and-such-a-time sign hanging in the window. But instead of numbers, different activities related to Emily filled each spot. And right now both hands pointed to "Quiet. Baby sleeping."

God, he missed…everything about them. With reverence, he eased open the front door. The scents of chocolate and fruit and spices wafted through the air, while the most beautiful woman in the world stood behind the counter, her blond hair up in a loose bun, her cheeks flushed, her white apron smeared with goodies, engrossed in helping old Mrs. Boot with her cookie selection.

"So that's two caramel crunchies," Bella whispered. "Four raspberry cobbler bars, seven black diamonds and an éclair, right?"

"I think that'll hold me and Ed till Monday," Mrs. Boot said in hushed tones.

"Four days?" Bella tipped up her chin as though she was thinking about that very hard. "I don't know." With a smile, she grabbed two more éclairs and put them in the bag. "On the house."

"Thank you, my dear." Mrs. Boot's gaze flickered toward the door and Michael. She grinned and said, "Can't tell if she's a devil or an angel."

"I have trouble with that myself," Michael whispered as he walked toward them.

Surprise lit Bella's blue eyes as she watched him approach. No doubt she wondered what he was doing here. And right now, he could hardly remember. All he wanted to do was take her in his arms and plant a kiss on her soft mouth.

Looking from one to the other, Mrs. Boot cackled softly, then made her way to the door, giving Michael an exaggerated wink. "Have a good afternoon."

When the old woman had gone, Bella looked at Michael and said professionally, "Can I help you, sir?"

But her clipped query didn't dissuade him. He'd been an ass the last time they'd been this close. She had a right to be angry with him.

He sidled up to the counter. "Once upon a time,

there was an amazing chocolate doughnut that a magical young lady made for me.'' He raised a dark brow. ''Ever heard of anything like that?''

''I might have,'' she said quietly.

''What'll it cost me to get one?''

She shrugged. ''I don't know. They're pretty special.''

''I'm not going to argue with you there.'' He gave her a half smile. ''How about a night out?''

''Excuse me?'' Guarded tone, guarded eyes.

''Dinner? Tonight? With me.''

Her lips parted, her eyes filled with uneasiness. ''I don't think so. I'm not really comfortable going back to your—''

''Not at the house. Here in town.''

Her brows drew together. ''I don't understand.''

''I thought we should celebrate,'' he continued. ''After all, you're the reason Micronics just doubled their offer for my software.''

''I'm what?'' she said as a hint of warmth lit her eyes.

''Those amazing ideas you gave me. I want to take you out and thank you properly.''

''Oh. Right.'' She looked down. ''Congratulations.''

She didn't sound pleased, and for a moment he wondered if he'd done the wrong thing coming here. But then his gaze found hers again, and he felt the need that had pulled him all the way back here from L.A.

''I miss you, Bella. Please.'' *Don't say no.*

For a long moment she didn't say anything, just stared at him. He was ready to call himself three kinds of idiot for baring his soul when she unexpectedly bent down and took something out of the display case.

When she stood back up again, a tentative smile graced her beautiful face, and a chocolate doughnut lay in her hand. She held it out to him. "Pick me up at seven?"

Nine

The mouthwatering scents of garlic, onions and grilled meat floated in the air. As Isabella sat across the rough-hewn table from Michael in the Fielding Supper Club—the *Gazette* had called it the best chop house this side of St. Paul—she tried to tell herself that this wasn't a date. That it was just a thank-you for helping him. But she couldn't stop wondering if maybe his tough shell was cracking a little. He'd probably never been "out on the town" in Fielding with anyone. Of course, "out on the town" in a burg this tiny wasn't saying much, but still, for him it was an unprecedented move.

And then there was the wonderful words he'd uttered, words that made her believe again that anything was possible.

He'd missed her.

Covertly, she abandoned her steak for a moment and stole a glance at him. He looked like a magazine cover in his black turtleneck sweater and jeans, a lock of black hair falling over one eye.

She mentally sighed and went back to her dinner. She'd missed him, too, and the ache had only deepened in the past weeks. It had been impossible to leave him when she had, yet somehow she'd found the strength. But today, when he'd walked into the bakery and looked at her with those mesmerizing eyes, she just hadn't been able to say no.

Maybe this dinner wasn't exactly a date, but Michael was here, in public, and all eyes were on him. And he'd chosen her to accompany him. It was a step in the right direction, a chance, a change. God help her, but she was going to cling to that.

"How's your steak?" he asked, cutting his own superbly grilled porterhouse.

"Wonderful." She glanced around the room at the watchful crowd, then back at him. "Listen, I don't think they'll stop unless you nod and smile at them. They probably don't think you're real."

"And what do you suppose they think I am?"

With a shrug she offered, "Alien, robot. You work with high-tech stuff. You know, rumors start."

"Yes, I do know," he said dryly. "I've had my share of rumors."

"Just give 'em a smile. Make their night."

On a chuckle, he looked up and waved. At first everyone just stared, then each in their turn gave him a return wave or a smile. When he finally brought his gaze back to her, his brow was furrowed.

"What's wrong?" she asked, taking a bite of her baked potato. "Not what you were expecting?"

"I don't know. I'm trying to avoid having expectations."

She smiled at that, took his newly acquired ease as another sign. Maybe if he came to town more often, he'd get to know some people, make some friends.

And see her.

She lifted her mineral water and saluted. "Congratulations again on landing another multimillion-dollar account."

"And to you, for having such amazing insights." His gaze warmed. "I couldn't have done it without you."

That look went straight through her, hitting every sensitive area she possessed. "Sure you could have. But thanks for the compliment."

He drank deeply from his glass of merlot. "Listen, Bella. In all seriousness, without your input, the deal wouldn't have been nearly as lucrative. I wanted to get you a gift, but I know how you feel about paybacks." He paused. "So, since she was the inspiration, anyway, I got Emily a gift." Michael handed Isabella a thick envelope. "I funded a tax-deferred education account for her."

Stunned, Isabella could do nothing but stare at the envelope. A college fund for Emily. It was something a father... She exhaled heavily. Her mind swam. How could she accept such generosity?

But before she could utter a word, he added, "It's for Emily, Bella. I want her to be able to go to the college of her choice. Let me do that for her."

The sincerity of his words tore at her. The wise part of her warned her to say thanks but no thanks. But the part that saw his need to do this couldn't refuse. She didn't know what else to say but, "Thank you, Michael."

He would be tied to them for life now, she thought as he nodded and returned to his meal. Did he understand that? And right now did she care?

If she had the magic eight ball that her father had given her for Christmas when she was ten, she was sure it would read, *Don't count on it.* Because even if this moment, or series of moments, was all there was, she didn't care. She'd take what she could get and let God handle the rest.

After all, He did work in mysterious ways.

When they finished dinner, Michael paid the bill and got their coats. "I forgot to congratulate you on the bakery," he said, holding out her navy wool Peacoat. "I noticed you don't have a sign yet. What are you going to call it?"

"I'm not." She laughed at his perplexed expression. "I'm leaving it up to Fielding. I placed a fishbowl on the counter and asked everyone to write down a name."

He shrugged into his leather jacket and grinned. "A smart businesswoman."

Her smile wide, she shook her head at him. "Letting people decide the name of the store is not just a business decision. I want them to feel like they're a part of the shop.''

"I like that,'' he said thoughtfully as they walked out of the restaurant.

Snowflakes fell from the night sky and the air was scented with holly. Christmas was coming, the time of year for happiness, cheer and goodwill toward men.

To this man, she thought with a smile. "So how was your first official dinner in Fielding?''

"How do you know it was my first?''

"Just a hunch,'' she said. "Was it all you imagined it to be?''

"More,'' he said dryly.

She laughed. "You think you might do it more often now?'' She mentally crossed her fingers.

"That depends.'' He stopped at the door to her shop. "You going to be there?''

"Maybe.'' There they were, so close. But a gap of uncertainty hung between them. "Would you like to come up and say good-night to Emily?''

He nodded. "Yes, I would.''

Michael felt like a world-class fool as he followed Isabella through the bakery and up the stairs. For some stupid reason, he'd hoped that seeing her for a few hours would cool his burning need to be with her. But it hadn't. It had only made him want her more.

Ruth greeted them at the door with a sleeping Emily in her arms. After a quick chat, she handed her off to Michael and left, saying she had to hurry home to watch Jay Leno with Thomas.

For Michael, seeing Emily was like coming home. After a month of caring for her, hearing her different cries, holding her, feeding her, he was due. But the little girl had something else on her mind, so he reluctantly handed her over to her mother.

"I should go and feed her," Bella said hesitantly. "Do you want to—"

"No. I'll stay here." If he was going to save this night from turning intimate, watching Bella nurse was out of the question.

She didn't leave immediately. He knew, because he could feel her eyes on him as he walked around the room, looking at her place. The changes she'd made since he'd last seen it were amazing. Her touch was everywhere. In the dried flowers, comfortable couches, brightly colored rugs, overflowing bookcase, smiling photographs of her and her father and Emily. It all had her signature. Homey, warm and incredibly inviting.

"Your leg bothering you tonight?" she asked, rocking Emily in her arms.

"Some." He turned to face her. "You don't happen to have a whirlpool on the roof or anything, do you?"

She shook her head. "Sorry."

The ache in his leg had turned raw about a half hour ago, but he'd pushed it out of his mind. In the past year, acute pain had started to accompany the ever-present ache. His doctors had said that there was nothing they could do. It came with age and weather. Move to California or Florida, they'd urged. That would probably be the wisest decision. But lately the idea of leaving the sleepy little town of Fielding had sounded more unpalatable than ever.

"Here's a thought," Bella said brightly. "I've got a nice big tub. Why don't I go and nurse Emily and you can soak in it for a while? We get really hot water here." She smiled slyly. "I'll even let you use my Epsom salts."

They were slipping back into comfortable as easily as a summer day on the porch. "I should probably head home."

She nodded, her eyes going lackluster. "All right."

"I should," he clarified, his gaze tightly knit with hers. "But I don't want to."

Her smile lit up the room. "I don't want you to, either. Salts are under the sink. I'll see you in a bit."

Michael refused to curse himself and his actions any more tonight. He wanted to be with her and she wanted to be with him. That had to be enough.

He found the salts, ran a hot bath, stripped, turned off the lights, leaving just the dim runners glowing as he settled down into the steaming tub. Heat surged into his muscles. His mind fell into blessed silence. He'd practically fallen asleep when he heard a knock and the bathroom door opening.

"I thought you might want a—" She stopped when she saw him, her eyes going wide. "I'm sorry, I…"

He slowly sat up, slightly drugged by the hot water.

"Thought I'd be fully clothed and maybe dunking the leg?"

"Something like that," she choked out, her nervous gaze moving from the floor back up to him.

He noticed that she'd changed into a set of totally unrevealing sweats. But damn, if she didn't look good enough to eat. "Emily asleep?"

"She's…out. Like a light." Clearing her throat, Bella asked, "So how's the leg?"

"Still tight." Just like the lower half of him.

Concern lit her eyes. "I could massage it for you."

He practically groaned. She was killing him here. Beneath the hot water, he was hard as granite. "No, it's fine."

"It's not fine," she said, walking toward him. "You just said—"

"I know what I said. Bella, don't—"

"Don't what?" She knelt beside the tub. "I just want to help."

He was done for. And if she touched him… "Believe me, being massaged by you would be a dangerous way to end our evening."

"You could think of me as a nurse," she offered.

"Not much better."

"Why don't you just lean back and let me help you?"

He cursed. But it wasn't his arousal that had him frowning as he lay back against the porcelain. It was the shame of her touching his leg, that imperfect, weak leg.

He was ready to call it quits when her gentle hands dipped into the water and found his thigh.

He groaned, his embarrassment forgotten.

"Too hard?" she asked, worry in her voice.

"No, it's good." He knew his eyes had gone to near black as he stared at her, his embarrassment now turning to desire. "Too good."

"I wish I could get a little closer," she said. "I'm in an awkward position—"

His movement was quick. He reached out, grabbed her waist, lifted her up and eased her down on top of him, sweats and all. Water splashed over the sides of the tub, splattered the floor.

"Close enough?" he growled, his mouth inches from hers.

She looked shocked at first, but then her lips parted. "You tell me," she whispered, pressing her hips against the solid length of him, then dragging a hand up the outside of his thigh.

He released a groan of pleasure. "I don't want to go back to my house, Bella."

"Tonight, you mean?"

"Tonight, tomorrow…" He cupped her face and kissed her mouth tenderly. "It's damned lonely up there."

She ran her tongue across his lower lip. "Then stay here."

That nearly undid him, but he managed to utter, "There'll be talk."

"Maybe a few moans, a sigh here and there, and hopefully later—"

"I meant from the town." He reached around and cupped her bottom.

"They're already talking."

"And you don't care?"

"No. I don't care."

His need to protect her in every way possible reared up. "Bella, there's one more thing I want to—"

Her fingers touched his lips, stopping him from saying anything more. "I know what you want and don't want, Michael Wulf. Now shut up and kiss me."

Ten

The bath grew cool too quickly.

Water splashed onto the already wet bathmat as Isabella pulled Michael out of the tub. Her eyes moved over him. Sleek and sexy and hard, he made her throat ache with want.

"I want to see you," he said as he stripped off her wet sweats. For a moment he simply took in the sight of her body glistening with moisture. She felt absolutely no embarrassment with him. And as her nipples beaded under his steely gaze, she stood taller, as though she needed to be as open as possible for him to be the same.

"You are so beautiful, Bella." Michael dipped his head and took one aching breast into his mouth.

Her fingers threaded through his hair and she pulled

him back up to face her. For fifteen years she'd had a crush on this man. And in a month and a half, that crush had grown into love. She knew what she wanted, and she was ready to take it, consequences be damned.

Impatience flooded her. "Do you want to take this slow?"

His eyes went black. "No."

"Good."

His weighty breath ended on a groaned, "I didn't bring any protection with me."

She grabbed his hand and tugged. "Follow me." She led him into her bedroom, straight to the chest at the foot of her cherry-wood sleigh bed. She opened the trunk, grabbed a small box and tossed it at him.

He caught it, then stared at her, his eyes burning a fever. "What are you doing with these?"

She pulled back her comforter and slid into bed. "They were in my hope chest, Michael." She raised a brow at him. "A girl can hope, right?"

His face broke out in a dangerous smile as he walked toward her. "And what exactly was this girl hoping for?"

Her pulse pounded at the base of her throat. "For Michael Wulf to get into her bed."

He was over her in seconds, his gaze penetrating her very soul, his hands fisted beside her shoulders. But only for a moment, only until she tipped up her chin and nipped his lower lip with her teeth.

Then the dam broke.

His mouth covered hers, took her rough and insistent while his hands ran up her body, feeling the curves of her hips, the fullness of her breasts in his palms.

Sweat broke out on his skin, hers too. He wanted to take his time, but he had none to offer. The scent of dried flowers mingled with the scent they made together, causing his mind to blur.

Under him, she bucked, pressing her core, wet and hot against his arousal, urging him to move with her.

He fought the reckless impulse to rise up and bury himself deep inside her, take her hard and fast. ''I don't want to hurt you, Bella,'' he said, breathing ragged.

With a sensual kiss, she wrapped her legs around his waist and arched, pressed. ''You won't.''

The brutal heat that burned between them demanded to be set free. Rising up, he slipped on a condom, then pushed slowly into her body.

A branding heat enveloped him.

Bella moaned, whispered against his skin, ''You're a perfect fit.''

Her words assaulted him, made his need to take and be taken swell. Dominated by something primal, Michael began to move, rise and lower, gentle strokes at first.

But Bella had other ideas.

Beneath him, her thrusts grew wild. Fast, a fevered pitch, that he couldn't help but match. Mind blank, body untamed, he gripped her hips and drove into her frantically, stroke after stroke until it was too much, until he went mad, until her lips parted, until she began to quake.

And when she cried out, when the walls of her womb gripped him tightly, a low, cavernous growl exploded in Michael's throat and he shuddered with her, hissed her name, then followed her into soul-shattering climax.

Against the lids of his eyes, insistent sunlight flashed. For a moment he wasn't sure where he was, just that he felt incredibly good. Then the events of the night before rolled across his mind like a lush carpet. He'd never held a woman through the night after making love. That action not only meant something to the woman, it meant something to him. Not exactly a commitment, but a relationship of sorts.

He and Bella had a relationship.

But what sort he wasn't sure.

He pulled her closer, then paused and opened his eyes. Clutched against his chest was one of Bella's pillows. She was gone.

The clock beside the bed blinked eight-fifteen, and he was alone. Cocking his head, he listened for Emily's cry or Bella's soft voice. But there was nothing. He ran a hand through his hair as his mind refocused.

Of course, it was Saturday morning—the bakery.

After dressing quickly, Michael made his way downstairs. He heard the din of hungry customers before he even reached the back door of the bakery. Bella would be swamped. Maybe he could help her out by watching Emily until the shop closed. Upstairs, where no one could see him, where no one would know that he'd spent the night here.

But his plan was quickly foiled when the double doors in front of him flew open, revealing a startled Bella and what appeared to be the entire town of Fielding.

If he'd expected Bella's expression to change into one of embarrassment, he'd probably have to wait all day. She smiled widely at him, said, "Oh, thank God," took his hand and led him behind the counter. "Today is the busiest it's ever been."

People had stopped talking, then resumed, just as they did when John Wayne walked into a saloon in one of those old westerns. And Michael didn't need to guess what the subject had changed to. But if Bella didn't mind, neither did he. It did a man good to know that a woman was proud of him.

And what a woman she was, he mused, taking in her fine, fine figure in a T-shirt, jeans and an apron that only partly obstructed his view. But it didn't matter. He knew firsthand what was under those clothes, how soft and warm her skin felt.

A soft gurgle caught his attention and he turned to see Emily cooing happily, touching her toes and smiling. She was in her playpen, tucked safely between two pillars, out of Bella's way, but still very much in viewing distance.

He turned to look at Bella, who was putting out a plate of doughnut samples on the counter. "Looks like you need a break."

"I'll be right with you," she told a customer at the

counter, then quick as lightning, she slipped something over Michael's head, pulled him down behind the counter and whispered, "What I need is *you*."

"Well, sweetheart, you got—" He glanced down. She'd put an apron on him. "What's this about?"

"Have I ever told you what magical hands you have?" she whispered, her eyes hopeful.

"No," he whispered back. "But I'd say it was probably implied. If we take those cries of pleasure—"

She put a finger to his lips and gave him a patient smile. "As I was saying, you really do have magical hands, Michael."

His brows rose, and so did the level of chatter in the bakery. "And you're sweet-talking me into...?"

"Taking orders, filling bags, making change."

"Anything else?" he asked dryly.

She looked up, probably checking to see if anyone had scaled the counter to hear them. "Be charming."

"I have no experience with that."

"You're a quick learner."

And she was so beautiful she made his hands itch. What was he supposed to do? Say no? He sighed and shook his head. "Damn you."

She laughed softly. "I owe you."

"Yeah, you do." He pulled her to him and kissed her soundly on the mouth. "And I'm collecting tonight."

With bright eyes and a brighter smile, she nodded. "I am your humble servant."

They both stood. Bella immediately started taking

an order, but Michael took a moment, easing a cramp out his leg before finally turning to face his nightmare. A gaggle of people clamoring to get freshly baked everything, trying to pretend they weren't feeling the curiosity written all over their faces.

The hours slipped by, fast and furious, and strangely, Michael actually started to enjoy himself. He'd done little but program computer software for the past fifteen years, and he had to admit it was kind of interesting to help run a small business. But mostly, it was just good to be around Bella. Every time he went into the storeroom to get more supplies, she'd follow him and they'd make out against the door for a few brief seconds.

When they returned, people would smile and chuckle. But she didn't care, so he didn't care. He wasn't afraid to admit she'd cast a spell over him.

When she went upstairs to feed Emily, he continued on with his duties and was surprised to find that the solo interaction with people wasn't so bad. They always offered him a friendly smile and a thank-you. A couple of people even asked what he was doing for Christmas and if he and Bella wanted to come for dinner some night. Not that he was ready to jump right into the fire just because he'd had a pleasant morning at the bakery. But it was surprisingly nice to be asked.

"So that was ten tarts, seven peanut-butter cookies, five double-chocolate-chip cookies, five regular chocolate-chip cookies, one loaf of pumpernickel bread thinly sliced and a Swedish Tea ring." He handed

Mrs. Trotsky her boxes and bags as Bella walked through the double doors holding Emily. "Do you need help out with that?"

The old woman tapped the shoulder of the man standing next to her. "Got my son here with me. But much obliged, Mr. Wulf."

"It's Michael," he said without thinking.

Mrs. Trotsky smiled. "I'm Bev and this is Harold."

Dammit. This socialization crap was all a result of Bella's spell. He clipped a nod at Mrs. Trotsky and her son, muttering, "Come again."

He felt Bella's gaze on him and turned, shooting her a wry glance. "Charming enough for you?"

She winked at him. "You're a natural."

"You're a virgin."

"What?" Michael exclaimed.

Isabella inched closer to him on the sofa as *Romancing the Stone* played on the television. "That's what you are, pal. A Saturday-night-movie-fest-pigout-spooning-on-the-couch-till-you-fall-asleep virgin."

He chuckled. "As much as you may think you just insulted me, Bella, you haven't. Even though I will admit that this—" he hugged the bowl of buttered popcorn to his chest protectively "—pursuit of fun is a first for me."

"Well, I like being your first." She smiled. "I still can't believe you haven't seen *Romancing the Stone*."

"I don't have time for—"

"Anything that's not related to business?" She snatched a piece of popcorn from his bowl and threw it at him.

He caught it and popped it into his mouth. "You trying to humanize me, Bella?"

"Oh, I'm doing my best."

He leaned in, and his mouth found her neck, searing hot kisses all they way to her ear. She shivered and he whispered, "Well, let it be said that I have the best-looking teacher in school. Lucky, lucky me."

Her eyes closed. "And don't you forget it."

"Not possible." His hand sneaked under her sweater. "Human contact is always the best place to start the humanizing process, don't you think?"

"Mmm," was all she could think to say as he nibbled her earlobe while his hand slid up her stomach, then slipped beneath her bra.

"What was that?" he whispered as he palmed her breast. "I didn't understand you."

Heat settled low in her belly and she pressed into his hand, wanting more. "I…said do you want to go into the bedroom?"

"Too far." Popcorn dropped to the floor as he pulled off her sweater in one easy movement, then unhooked her bra.

Gunshots rang out over the TV, but all Isabella heard was the humming of her body, on fire and filled with need. Michael's mouth found her neck, searing slow kisses down, down until he reached her breast.

"Michael," she rasped as he flicked the sensitive bud with his tongue.

"Tell me, Bella." His hand slipped inside her jeans, under the panties. "Tell me how this makes you feel."

His fingers dipped low, stroking her cleft until she couldn't breathe, couldn't think. She spoke through senses only. "Hot and shaky, like fireflies trying to get free…" It could've been gibberish, but it was all she could offer.

She felt his hand leave her, felt him take her with him as he stood up. Her eyes opened to his gaze, so tender.

"Bella…" He wanted to say more—she could see it in his eyes—but he didn't. Instead, he unbuttoned her jeans and slid them down.

With shaky hands, she pulled off his sweater and jeans. When she stood before him once again, she ran her hands up his chest possessively, over the muscle, feeling his heart slamming against his ribs. Her gaze flew to his, his eyes so hot it almost made her step back. Lord, he made her crazy. She wanted this, wanted him forever. But the best she could hope for now was to show him.

She pushed him down on the spacious couch and straddled him.

He growled with surprise. "It looks like you have another assignment planned for tonight, Teacher." His eyes remained on her as his hands once again searched out the wet heat he'd created.

"I've planned a test," she uttered through breaths.

"A test?"

"Of stamina." She moved against his fingers, against the steely length of him. "Mine outlasting yours."

At that challenge, Michael released her and flipped her onto her back. "Oh, sweetheart. You don't stand a chance."

She smiled up at him. "I was hoping you'd say that."

He sat up for a moment, reached down to retrieve a foil packet from his discarded jeans. "I came prepared this time."

"Can I do it?" Isabella heard the shyness in her query, but she reveled in her boldness. It was love, pure and simple, that made her request such an intimacy.

Leaning toward her, he kissed her lips softly. "Yes."

With tentative fingers, she opened the packet. Michael drew in a breath as she slowly moved the latex down his manhood, then groaned as she wrapped her hands around him and guided him to the apex of her thighs.

Deep longing filled his gaze as he hovered at the entrance to her body. In that moment, as their eyes met, Isabella wanted to tell him that she loved him, that she wanted this forever, that with him she felt complete. But when he pushed into her, all she could understand were sensations.

He moved inside her slowly at first, then faster. She wanted to hold on to the sweet heat of the moment, but it was no use. Gasping, she fought for breath and for her sanity as that delicious heat spread through her core. The speed of his thrusts increased to a pitch where nothing existed but the two of them. It was madness, a thirst that needed to be quenched.

She cried out as orgasm hit, but Michael continued to thrust over and over as her walls clenched and tightened. Then he stiffened, a primal groan tearing from his throat.

"Bella…" He thrust into her again and again before their bodies finally cooled and their breathing returned to normal.

Rolling to the side, he took her with him so that they faced each other on the roomy sofa. Michael touched her cheek, kissed her lips softly, then pulled her close.

"You're mine," he whispered, caressing her back in long, easy strokes.

She shivered, but hardly felt it. His words spoke directly to her heart, making her wonder if…

"Tonight you're all mine."

A wave of disappointment poured through her. Michael was talking about right now, not the future. It wasn't the dream she longed for, but she sure wouldn't let that truth kill this time between them. She'd known the rules going in, and she was not about to play the dejected lover now.

"You think you got more in ya, Wulf?" Her tone was teasing.

A smile tugged at the corners of his mouth. "More tasting your sweet nipples until they harden in my mouth? More feeling you grow wet against my fingers?" As he spoke she felt him begin to grow hard against the apex of her thighs. "More pushing into your body while you wrap your legs around me?" With a devilish smile, he pushed inside her. "Is that what you mean, Ms. Spencer?"

She gasped and draped her leg over his hip, giving him full access. And as all thoughts and questions and wishes drifted from her mind, she whispered, "You win."

Eleven

She slept like an angel.

Michael had noticed that once before. Under the same moon on the night she'd first come to his house. He'd sat in his chair beside the fire, watching over her, wondering what dreams filled her mind as he kept his distance.

Just like now, he mused, folding his hands across his chest and leaning back in the desk chair he'd occupied for more than thirty minutes. After he'd made love to Bella a second time on the couch, she'd fallen asleep in his arms. Content just to lie there with her, he'd watched the last few minutes of the movie, then the screen had filled with snow as the VCR shut itself off. Finally he'd carried her to bed and tucked her in.

He'd wanted to go with her, slip beneath the sheets and pull her close. But tonight he knew he didn't dare.

Something had changed. He couldn't put his finger on it, but there was something inside him tonight that begged for release. Perhaps it was a need for more—more of Bella, more connection with this town, more freedom from his solitude. Whatever it was, it had surfaced this weekend in Fielding.

He knifed a hand through his hair. He needed to go back where he belonged before he was sucked into a vortex of certain disappointment. Before he began to believe he belonged to a woman, a child and a community.

But although he could readily leave the town behind when this weekend was over, Bella and Emily were a different story. If Bella was willing, he wanted her and Emily to come home with him. For as long as they wanted to be there. No strings, no promises, just being together.

It was all he could offer, all he was willing to risk. He hoped it was enough.

From the baby monitor beside the bed, he heard Emily begin to fuss. As though she heard her child in her sleep, Bella stirred. She was exhausted, getting up before dawn to bake, serving customers all day and taking care of Emily. Such a rigorous schedule was another solid reason for her to come live with him. He could give her some slack. Thank God she had the good sense to close the bakery on Sundays. Most everyone in town had gotten their provisions today, and Bella could use a full night's sleep.

Emily's fussing strengthened into soft cries. Michael got up, turned down the monitor and threw on his pants, then quietly left the room.

Still decorated with rosebud wallpaper and lace curtains from when a young Bella had occupied it, the only difference in Emily's room was the baby furniture. In the center of the long space a crib was set up atop a plush pink rug, and a mobile of stars and moons hung over it.

"Not tired, either, princess?" he whispered, picking her up and holding her against his chest. "Ah, it's more of a diaper issue, huh?"

Emily mewed softly.

"I'll take that as a yes." He placed her down on the changing table. It was old hat to him now, he realized: talking to her, making faces, giving her those plastic keys she liked to bite on when she was being changed.

After Emily had a clean diaper, Michael rocked her for a few minutes, then tried putting her back in her crib. But the little girl was having none of it. When her back hit the mattress, her round face scrunched up and a wail escaped her lips.

"I'm a little hungry myself," he said, gathering her up in his arms once again. "Let's go see what your mom's got in the fridge."

Several bottles of expressed breast milk lined one shelf of the refrigerator. Michael placed Emily in her baby seat, then heated up one of the bottles. After testing its temperature, he dropped into a chair, cuddled the baby close and gave her the bottle.

She took to it at once, and Michael settled back against the chair and exhaled. Never in his life had he felt so relaxed. Emily stared up at him with wide trusting eyes, making him feel that strange sense of belonging again.

"You're trouble," he told her softly. "Bella's got her work cut out with you."

She blinked up at him.

He chuckled softly. "But I'm guessing there's no sweeter work to be had."

Only the sound of Emily suckling filled the house. He couldn't take his gaze off that cherubic face. And as her eyes drifted closed, he could only whisper, "You're both lucky to have each other."

He knew he must sound like an idiot, talking to a six-week-old baby in a dim kitchen in the middle of the night. But he wanted her to know, to always know, that people loved her and felt fortunate to have her.

And hell, no one was up to hear his foolishness, anyway.

No one but Isabella, that is.

She stood in the living room watching and listening, her breath held, her heart balancing somewhere between wonder and sadness. To anyone who saw what she was seeing, Michael Wulf looked like Emily's father. They were so natural together, the calmness he brought out in her and the softness she brought out in him.

Love surged into her heart. And it seemed quite clear that she wasn't the only one who was taken with him. Her daughter had fallen in love with Michael, too.

Feeling as though she was trespassing on sacred ground, Isabella returned quietly to her bedroom. But the love in her heart sent questions rocketing through her mind. Did Michael Wulf have any clue how much they both needed him? How much they loved him?

And if he didn't, should she tell him?

Anxieties tripped across her heart as she slipped into bed, then, out of habit, reached over to the monitor and turned up the volume.

"...and he has a long white beard, a red suit and a whole herd of reindeer that can fly." She heard Michael's deep chuckle. "I know what you're thinking. It seems scientifically impossible. But with the power of magic, Emily, anything's possible."

Anything's possible.

Isabella clutched the pillow to her chest and sighed. She knew exactly what kind of magic she was going to ask Santa for this year.

At seven a.m., Isabella awoke, content and happy to feel Michael's warm chest beneath her cheek. He'd come to bed late last night, but when he had, she'd snuggled close to him, sighing when he put his arm around her and gathered her to him possessively. Only then had she truly been able to sleep.

She'd dreamed of more weekends like this one, with no Sundays to put an end to her happiness. But that was just a dream. Sometime today he would put on his expensive coat, call for an expensive car and leave.

But it was not today yet.

Shamelessly trying to rouse him, Isabella eased her leg across his hips. He stirred, but didn't awake. Lightly she touched his taut stomach, running her hand up the delicious column of hair, threading her fingers in the thick of it. Need coursed through her veins. Every inch of her, inside and out, craved him. It was so unusual for her to want a man so desperately, body and soul, but Michael Wulf wasn't just any man.

She had a few more hours of showing him just how much she loved him. That was all she was guaranteed.

Bypassing subtlety, she pressed her hips against him and moved her hand downward.

Michael's first thought was that he was dreaming— a hell of a delicious dream, too. But then he felt Bella's hand on him, felt her tongue dart out and lave his nipple, and he knew that this was all heaven-sent reality. He was hard as granite in Bella's small hand, and so turned on he could barely remember his name.

Night and day, the woman bewitched him.

And he loved every minute of it.

He let his predatory hands explore everything they could reach—her back, her buttocks, her breasts. His eyes remained closed, but he heard her urgent moans, felt her hips thrusting insistently against his thigh.

''Michael, please…'' she uttered, her tone needful and feverish.

Enough playtime. He was awake.

He rolled her to her back, quickly put on protection, then plunged into her. A very satisfied gasp escaped her lips as warm wet heat closed all around him. He couldn't bear to leave her, but knowing the pleasure that would come from it, he rose, hovered at the entrance to paradise, then drove home once again.

"Wrap your legs around me, sweetheart," he instructed, and she instantly did as he asked.

The fevered longing that zipped through his body was so foreign, but so welcome. This connection was a first. The feeling that rushed over him with every stroke made his mind falter, his will weaken.

"I can't hold on," she whispered, dragging her hands down his back, gripping his buttocks.

He groaned. "Take what you want, Bella. Everything you want."

Smiling up at him, she used her hands to pull him deeper. Their eyes remained locked on each other's. It was a lost cause, but as they moved fitfully together, he fought to separate his physical needs from the emotional wants.

She fit him so perfectly, and even though he chose not to give it a name, what he felt for her was undeniable, uncontrollable and totally unstoppable.

Shots of honey-sweet pleasure ripped through him. He dragged in a breath, just as Bella gave a cry and shuddered around him, her muscles gripping him. All thoughts abandoned him.

Out of control and out of his mind, he quickened his strokes, slamming into the center of her where liquid heat resided.

With her soft moans in his ear, he couldn't fight any longer. He didn't *want* to fight any longer. Thunder hit, lightning crashed and he plunged over the edge.

Isabella stood in the center of town, Emily in her arms, Michael by her side, and took in the view. It had been years since she'd seen Fielding dressed up for the holidays, and it was as alive with spirit as it had always been. From the silver bells, handmade ornaments, flocked trees that gave off that wondrous scent of pine, green holly and ivy, and strings of colored lights to the adults and children with that Norman Rockwell look of excitement and anticipation on their faces.

Christmastime was here.

And she wanted to enjoy it for a moment before they started their—

"Christmas shopping, Bella?" Michael raised a brow at her.

She laughed and said wryly, "It's a new concept for you, I know."

He shot her a mock frown. "You're becoming too damn sassy."

With a quick smile, she started down the street. "Thank you. I try." The town truly looked picture-postcard perfect. The sun was shining, the park benches and street lamps had a light dusting of snow, windows were filled with treasures, people waved at one another and children's laughter filled the air.

"Have you given any thought to what you'd like

for Christmas, Michael?'' Isabella asked. *Maybe one more night with me?*

"Peace," he said.

"As in 'peace on earth'?"

"Nope. As in 'peace and quiet.'''

She turned around and gave him a patient smile. "Listen, if you're going to hang out with me and Emily, any and all Scrooge and Grinch references are strictly prohibited."

"Fine." He tipped his chin down. "You're going to make me pick out a tree, too, aren't you?"

"Not until later." She laughed at his beleaguered expression, then the display in the shop window in front of her caught her gaze. "Look at this."

Imitation snow framed the window, setting off the little scene inside perfectly. A handmade train carried angels, nativity figurines, wooden Santas and presents along its little black tracks.

"This is the sweetest, most wonderful time of the year." She glanced over her shoulder at Michael. "Are you really going to tell me that you don't like any of it?"

"All right," he acquiesced with a grumpy huff. "There is one thing."

Isabella regarded him with curious eyes. "Well, don't keep me in such suspense."

He leaned in and kissed her ear. "I happen to be particularly fond of mistletoe. But don't spread that around."

Despite the warmth of her wool coat, a shiver ran down her spine. Since coming home to Fielding, her life had been a series of perfect moments. Standing on the sidewalk, being kissed by the man she loved—in the town she loved—was certainly another.

And God help her, she refused to accept that this perfect time, this perfect weekend, was swiftly coming to a close.

"Your secret's safe with me," she said, forcing a lightness she didn't feel into her tone. "But I can't vouch for Emily."

Michael looked down and brushed the baby's cheek with his thumb. "You won't tell anyone, will you, princess?"

Emily gurgled. Isabella interpreted. "She says no problem. Not until she starts talking, anyway."

"Clever girl." He straightened and put on a game smile. "All right, I'm ready for this shopping expedition. Where are we headed?"

"Let's go in here," she said, nodding at the craft shop. "I want to pick out Emily's first ornament."

He looked up at the sign. "The Crafty Corner? Can't these people come up with something more original?"

She glared at him. "Give 'em a break, okay, Wulf?"

"For you, Bella, I'll give everyone a break." He winked at her. "Today."

"Oh, the generosity," she said on a chuckle as they walked into the store.

Within two minutes Bella was deeply involved in a discussion on how to make a gilded angel for the top of the tree, and Michael was walking around the store wondering what sort of gifts to get Bella and Emily for Christmas. Sure, he'd only celebrated Christmas once, but if the two of them were going to be at his house, he wanted to do the holiday up right, with all the trimmings and loads of presents.

Out of the corner of his eye he spotted a wall of little handmade ornaments. If Bella was going to get Emily one, maybe he'd get one for Bella, he thought, walking to the back of the store where the huge array hung on wooden pegs. He smiled as he spotted the perfect ornament. Hanging from a red-and-white checked ribbon was a miniature pan like the ones Bella used for baking with two miniature gingerbread men on it.

"I'm just telling you, Joan, I don't buy this big change that Michael Wulf has supposedly undergone."

Michael froze, the ornament forgotten. To his left, the stockroom door stood partially open. His jaw tight as a trap, he glanced inside. Molly Homney, hands planted on ample hips, stood above a young woman who was methodically unpacking nativity figures from a box.

"Isabella seems very happy," Joan said.

Molly snorted. "Well, of course she does. She's in love with him."

Michael's chest tightened painfully, his mind rewinding what he'd just heard. Bella? In love with him?

"She can't tell her backside from her elbow right now," Molly continued. "But I can."

Joan sighed. "And what do you see?"

"Trouble. That man is used to living in a cave. And he can survive that way. But can Isabella? Can Emily?"

Cocking her head to one side, Joan said thoughtfully, "Maybe they could get married and live in town."

Molly shook her head. "I've said it before and I'll say it again. It's not the house that Michael Wulf lives in that makes him uncivilized. It's his attitude. He and Isabella could live anywhere and he would still sneer at the world." A look of pure pity crossed her face. "Just think about little Emily growing up that way. No friends." On a sigh, she added, "And Isabella has just come home. Such a shame..."

Michael didn't want to hear any more—didn't need to hear any more. He turned and walked away, pure unadulterated anger roaring through his blood. But it wasn't directed at the town's resident gossip. It was directed at himself. Why the hell hadn't he thought about how his way of life would affect Emily and Bella?

Because he wanted to be with them at all costs, that was why.

Just then, Bella caught his eye and motioned for him to come over to the register. Was Molly right? he wondered as he walked toward her. Did Bella love him? Could a man so incapable of love see such a thing in the eyes of another?

"Doesn't this angel look just like Emily?" Bella said, thrusting the angel-kit package at him and switching her daughter to her other arm. "I thought this would be so cute on top of the tree for her first Christmas."

Struggling for control, Michael looked at it. "It's great."

"I'm not all that crafty." Her voice was filled with enthusiasm. "But I'm willing to suffer through a few mistakes as long as it comes out all right in the end."

Guilt constricted his chest, heavy and imposing, and he forced his gaze to hers. Those magnetic sapphire eyes were filled to the brim with happiness. But love? He wasn't sure what love looked like. Still, there was a certain softness when she looked at him.

What kind of man was he, bringing her into his life, his tortured little world?

He was a selfish bastard, that's what he was.

He raked a hand through his hair. He'd take this last day of holiday cheer, but then he had to give them up. Even if it killed what was left of his heart, he was going to make sure that he protected Bella and Emily from the town's nosy speculation—and from himself.

In front of the bay window in her living room sat the most beautiful tree Isabella had ever seen.

Across the candlelit dinner table, she stared at the blue spruce Michael had picked out, dragged home, then set up while she made dinner. He'd been a bit distant when they'd left the Crafty Corner, but she'd just chalked that up to his being holiday-unfamiliar and coaxed him back into the spirit in time for their tree-buying excursion.

Or, actually, Emily had. She'd been crying when they'd gotten to the tree lot, but as soon as Michael had taken her in his arms, that crying had turned into cooing. Quite proud of himself, Michael had told Isabella to follow him, that he and Emily were going to pick out the biggest and the best tree in the lot, even if they had to cut a hole in the ceiling to make it fit. The enthusiastic gesture had instantly reminded her of her father.

"Remember the Christmas you spent here with me and Dad?" Isabella said, taking the last bite of her roast pork.

He nodded, a forkful of apple stuffing on the way to his mouth. His eyes were hooded. "Yes."

"The scent of pine filling the house, the naked tree just waiting for its dressing."

"You didn't decorate until Christmas Eve, right?"

She smiled. "Dad's tradition." She pointed to the base of the tree. "And there's Mom's tradition. She made that tree skirt the year I was born."

He glanced over his shoulder. "It's beautiful." When he turned back to face her, his eyes had softened. "I know that's really important to you, Bella."

"What?"

"Family. Traditions."

She took a sip of sparkling cider. "It is. And even more so now that I have Emily. I really feel that it's important to give a child a sense of her history, of the memories that made her home what it is, you know?"

Michael chuckled bitterly. "I don't think a child would be interested in *my* history or my memories."

His words stung. Isabella felt as though he'd just taken a giant step backward, and she didn't know why.

"Well, there's always room to make some new ones," she offered quickly. "You could spend Christmas here with Emily and me. Just like old times, but with new memories."

Silence filled the pine-scented air until Michael cleared his throat. "I appreciate the offer, Bella. But I won't be in Fielding for Christmas."

Isabella's heart dipped in her chest. "Where will you be?"

"Los Angeles. I'm going back to work with Micronic's programmers to customize the software."

She just stared at him, trying to read what was behind those steel-gray eyes. But they gave away nothing. In fact, they looked exactly the way they had the day he'd left Fielding as a boy, the way they had the first few days she'd stayed at his house. "You're really going to work over Christmas?"

"No. I'm actually going to stay and check out a few houses in the area."

It was as though the breath had been sucked out of her lungs. For him to go away on business for a few weeks stank, but the possibility of his moving away...

"Something for winter," he continued unemotionally. "The climate should be easier on my leg."

Forcing herself to swallow the Sahara in her throat, Isabella tried not to show the intensity of the pain in her heart. "Well, if you're back for New Year's, Emily and I could come and pick you up at the airport. We could go—''

''I'm not really sure how long I'm staying in California,'' he said quickly, dropping his napkin onto the table beside his plate.

She tried to bite her tongue, to keep the desperation she felt out of her tone, but she couldn't seem to stop the words from coming. ''Do you know where you'll be staying when you do come back?''

He leaned forward in his chair and said quietly, ''Bella, this isn't the way I live. And nothing's going to change that.''

Tears pricked at her eyes. ''Living without love is not living, Michael.''

''To me, it is.''

''I really thought that maybe this weekend you saw something different.''

''I did see something.''

She shook her head. ''But?''

His eyes softened. ''Did you really think that after a few dinners in town, a couple of days helping out in the bakery and a little Christmas shopping, I would all of sudden become Joe Citizen?''

''No, Michael.'' Past tears now, she pressed on. She had words to say, words she'd been sitting on far too long. No doubt, they would fall on deaf ears, but if she had any hope of moving on with her life, Michael Wulf needed to know the truth in her heart. ''I hoped that you would want a life with Emily and me.'' With every ounce of courage she had left, she met his gaze. "I hoped that you would learn to love me the way I love you."

A muscle jumped in his jaw as he stared at her. For a moment she imagined she saw something akin to tenderness in his shadowed gaze, but it was gone in an instant.

"That's not possible for me."

She nodded slowly, her heart breaking silently, the tiny sharp fragments of it scattering like dust. "All right, Michael."

"But as for a friendship—"

She held up her hand. "That's not possible for me." She came to her feet. "I'm going to check on my daughter. Please be gone by the time I get back."

On legs made of water, Isabella turned and left the room. It was like walking in mud. Each step felt heavy, each breath caught as she tried to hold off the wrenching sob that ached to escape her throat.

Nothing had prepared her for this—this mind-numbing moment when she walked away from the love of her life, knowing that her dream of being with him, of having him love her, had just died.

But with a determination she hadn't known she possessed, she did just that.

Twelve

"Ladies and gentlemen, in preparation for our descent, please put away all electronic devices and fasten your seat belts. We will be landing in Minneapolis just before noon. Weather is looking promising for Christmas Eve. Mild windchill and a light snowfall. Happy holidays, everyone, and thank you for flying Northern Airlines."

Michael shut his laptop computer.

What was he supposed to do now? For the past two weeks, work had been the only thing that had kept him from thinking. About Bella, Emily and the damned holidays.

He stared out the tiny window. Tonight was Christmas Eve. The night when Santa zipped down the chimney and gave presents to all the good girls and boys. Well, he'd never been a good boy. And the only presents he wanted were ones he couldn't have.

The plane began its descent into the Minneapolis/ St. Paul airport, and Michael cursed the shot of excitement that rippled through him. He wasn't going to see her. He was going back to that empty glass fortress. The one he'd built to keep the world out.

But Bella's face could haunt him there just as easily as it had in California. He couldn't work every moment, no matter how hard he tried. So whenever he was out, driving or eating, she and Emily would trample into his mind, mess up his sanity again. Whenever he saw a baby with those plastic keys or the book with the fuzzy bunny on the cover, his heart would lurch for Emily. When he fell into bed at night, he wanted Bella beside him. And when he went house-shopping, he couldn't help but wonder what she would think of the place. Especially the kitchen. Would she like it? Could she create in there?

Rubbing a hand over his face, he groaned. He was a fool. He had once again realized that being miles away had only made him want her more. But there was nothing to do except wait it out, let time heal if it could. All he had to do was overcome that feeling of loneliness, that need, that incredible ache. Hell, he'd gotten over it with his parents. He'd do it again.

The plane touched down on the tarmac smoothly, then rolled to a stop. Around him, passengers jolted to their feet, grabbing bags and brightly wrapped packages from the overhead bins before filing out of the plane and rushing down the jetway. They were all, no doubt, anxious to see their loved ones, their families, anxious to start the holiday.

Michael took his time. He had no driver waiting for him this time. He hadn't wanted to steal someone away from their family on Christmas Eve to drive him home. It was easy just to rent a car.

But when he stepped into the terminal, he saw that he didn't have to. "What the hell are you doing here?"

Walking toward him, Thomas chuckled. "Well, that's just fine. I come all the way out here to pick you up, bring you back where you belong, and this is the thanks I get."

Had he told Thomas when he'd be getting in today? Michael wondered, trying to ignore how good it felt to have the man here. "Thanks, Thomas, but you shouldn't have come. Tonight's Christmas Eve and your family—"

"My family is fine. They're expecting me for dinner." Side by side, they walked down the concourse. "Don't tell me you'd rather have some strange limousine driver than a friendly face."

"That depends."

"On what?"

"If that friendly face is going to give me a lecture all the way home."

"Now what in the world would I have to lecture you about?" Thomas asked breezily. "You seem to be doing just fine."

"I am." Michael sounded way too convincing, even to his own ears.

"That's wonderful. Business is good?"

They passed through the double doors and stepped out into a brisk winter afternoon. "Very good, in fact."

"And I must say you look healthy as a jackass."

"Don't you mean 'as a horse'?" Michael asked dryly.

"No. I mean jackass."

Shaking his head, Michael followed him to the car. "This is the beginning of that lecture, right?"

"There's not going to be anything like that." Thomas opened the trunk and waited while Michael dropped his bags in. "No questions, no comments, no offering information on certain people in town. Nothing."

Michael didn't answer right away. They were in the car, heading onto the highway before he couldn't stand it anymore. "All right, I'll bite. How are they?"

"Who?"

"Now which one of us is being the jackass?" Michael chuckled. "Bella and Emily. How are they doing?"

"They're doing beautifully. Emily is sweet and growing bigger every day."

Michael felt a strange little ping in the region of his heart. He'd missed almost two weeks of her life. "And Bella?"

"Isabella's business is booming and she has her friends around her. She seems happy enough. She and Emily are coming to the house tomorrow for Christmas dinner. My wife is making ham *and* turkey this year, and of course her sage and onion stuffing. Kyle and Derek are going to be there, too." He tossed Michael a sly glance. "You know, I think my eldest might have a crush on Isabella."

Michael frowned. "What?"

The doctor shrugged. "Derek *was* the one who called and asked her to come."

Anger seeped through Michael like an oil slick. What was she thinking, accepting Derek's invitation? She just had a baby—she wasn't ready to get involved. And Derek Pinta was…was… Oh, hell he was exactly the kind of man Michael wasn't. Upstanding, sociable, popular and mild-natured, a real citizen of the world.

Dammit, he had no claim on Bella, no right even to want one. But the thought of her with another man made him nuts, and that man being a father to his—

He stopped that thought midstride. He was no husband to Bella, and Emily wasn't his child. It didn't matter if he wanted that status changed. They deserved better than a defeated beast with a wounded leg and a caged heart.

Isabella turned her sign to "Mother and Child Done for the Day."

She'd sold every last one of her silver bells, gingerbread men and red-nosed Rudolphs, and even though her adrenaline was still pumping, it was time to call it quits.

In the past couple of weeks, it hadn't been difficult to move through those mad hours of early rising, baking, filling orders and caring for Emily. The activity had kept her mind occupied—and off Michael Wulf. A little trick she'd learned from him. Work was the answer to all ills, apparently.

At night, she'd be so exhausted that she'd just fall into bed and into a dreamless sleep. And she'd awake before the sun each morning and do it all again. She ran on batteries, it seemed, quite unaware of the world around her at times.

Except for her time with Emily, she thought, picking up her daughter and carrying her upstairs. Those were the magical times. Cuddling, reading to her, playing on the little ducky blanket that Michael had given them.

Then her mind would lose its blessed numbness and fly to him again. What was he doing? Did he ever think of her? When was he coming back? *Was* he coming back?

A strong hand fisted around her heart and squeezed, but she fought it. She had to. If it was just her, she could crawl under the covers and stay there for a week. But it wasn't just her. She had Emily to think of.

Gently, Isabella placed Emily on the changing table and grabbed a clean diaper.

She looked down at her daughter. These thoughts, this aching heart, all were dangerous. She would never get over Michael, she knew that. But for her daughter's sake, she had to find a way to keep trying.

Tonight her friends were coming over for a girls' gab session, and she would put on a brave face, tell

Molly again that she didn't know where Michael was and change the subject.

She sure wasn't about to tell them the truth. How she'd told him to go. Not because she didn't love him, but because she loved him too much to pretend she didn't want more than friendship. And that for a short time, whether he'd wanted to admit it or not, they'd been so much more.

They'd been a family.

"We'll have to hurry," Thomas said as he pulled up alongside the curb and switched off the engine. "It's going to be dark soon."

Michael's hand gripped the car-door handle as his mind rioted over what to do next. This stop at the cemetery had been his idea. But as for the purpose, he wasn't exactly sure.

Thomas put a hand on his shoulder. "Do you want me to go with you?"

"No."

"All right."

"I don't know why I'm here."

"Sure you do," Thomas said gently. "You want to wish Emmett a merry Christmas and ask him if he thinks you're worthy of his daughter."

Michael turned to look at Thomas. "I know I'm not worthy."

"Why do you think that?"

"I don't want to... It's just that..." What? Why couldn't he put a name to this feeling? Why was he so damn afraid?

"You love her."

"Yes." The word came out in a rush. He stilled, letting it seep in, trying to understand how loving anyone was possible for a man like him. But it was true. He loved her. So much he ached with it. And he realized it now. Now, when it was too late. "I love her, Thomas. And that's exactly why I can't have her."

"Excuse my French, but that's crap."

"You know who I am, Thomas. *How* I am. I can't be a part of this town, part of life. I'm no good at it."

"Again, crap."

Frustrated, Michael banged his fist on the side of the door. "Bella and Emily need that good, upstanding citizen type who smiles and shouts hello to his neighbors every morning." He chuckled bitterly. "I know how to shout, but I barely know how to smile."

"Look at me," Thomas demanded, and Michael grudgingly did as he asked. "Do you want Isabella and Emily? Do you want them to be your family?"

"God, yes."

"Then you'll learn how to smile, Michael Wulf."

He snorted. "Simple as that?"

"Most everybody in this town has their arms out to you. They want to give you a chance." Thomas's gaze softened. "After what you've been through, I don't blame you for the doubt that's in your heart. But when's it going to end?"

Michael turned back to the window, to his view of the cemetery. "I'm not sure it *can* end."

"Michael," the old man said, reaching out his

gnarled hand and laying it on the smooth wool of Michael's overcoat. "It's time to let go. You have to want them enough to let go of your demons."

Outside, snow fell so softly against the tombstones that Michael almost felt he could hear them whispering.

He had to admit it to himself, let himself feel the truth. There was nothing he wanted more than Isabella and Emily. Nothing. He loved her, loved her child, and he'd squash a thousand demons to have a chance to show them how deep his love ran. If she would still have him.

Ever since his parents had taken off and left him, he'd declined to participate in the game of life and he'd blamed the world. His fear of being discarded again by someone he loved had imprisoned him, had made him take what he'd heard from Molly Homney and use it as a shield.

Bella had opened the door to life and showed him what could be, what he could have. She'd shown him heaven and he'd chosen the comfort of hell.

No more.

Michael opened the car door, got out and walked over to the grave of Emmett Spencer, beloved husband and father, and said the words that would change him forever.

"I love your daughter."

"I need more popcorn," Connie said, holding up her long string of popcorn and cranberry swag for the tree.

"Why did she get the food decoration," Molly moaned, "and I get stuck with construction-paper links?"

April Young rolled her eyes. "Because no one trusts you with a needle."

Wendy snorted. "No one trusts you with the popcorn and cranberries."

Everyone laughed, even Molly. Rid of their husbands, significant others and children for a few hours, the fivesome from high school had fallen easily into their old ways. Sitting around the coffee table, they'd scarfed down all the food they'd brought and talked about old times and old boyfriends.

It was fun and truly lovely, but Isabella's mind was elsewhere. Thank goodness her friends had steered clear of discussions about Michael Wulf. She appreciated them for that and so did her heart.

"I'll make some more popcorn," Isabella announced, coming to her feet.

But before she could get halfway to the kitchen, there was a knock at the door.

"Did you invite some boys, Isabella?" Connie asked with a grin.

Wendy clasped her hands together. "Ooh, I heard Ronnie Mills has a crush on you. And he just got his braces off."

Isabella grinned at the schoolgirl sound of that as she walked to the door.

"Maybe it's a stripper," April offered, and they all laughed.

But it was no stripper.

Looking incredibly handsome in a black sweater, gray pants and his long black coat, Michael Wulf leaned against the door and smiled. "Hi, Bella."

The room behind her fell dead silent, but Isabella could hear her heart battering against her chest. It seemed as though she hadn't seen him in years, not weeks. Her longing for him surged to the surface like a fisherman's bobber.

"You're home," she said inanely, her cheeks growing instantly warm. "I mean, you're back from California."

His gaze roamed over her, drinking her in, unnerving her jumbled nerves. "I couldn't stay away. Not from Fielding or—"

"Your glass house?" The bitter tone was uncontrolled. Why did he have to come here and torture her?

"Can I come in?"

It took every ounce of self-control she had to say, "I have friends over. Maybe some other time—"

Ignoring her protest, he stepped past her into the apartment. "This can't wait." He nodded at her friends. "Hello, ladies."

They all mumbled hellos, then turned their gazes back to what they were doing.

"I'm sorry to interrupt the evening," he said, "but I have something to tell Bella that just can't wait."

Connie stood up. "We should probably go—"

"No. You all—" he looked pointedly at Molly and she blushed "—need to hear this."

Isabella found her voice. "Michael, what's going on?"

He turned to face her again, his gray eyes softer than she'd ever seen them. "I had a conversation with your father today."

Her heart lurched. "You went to the cemetery?"

He nodded.

"Why?"

"I needed to tell him something." He reached for her hand, lifted it to his mouth and kissed it softly. "I love you, Bella."

Eyes wide, she just stared at him. "You what?"

"He said he loves you," April said. Connie quickly shushed her.

Isabella hardly heard her friends. Her mind was reeling, her heart pounding. "But you told me—"

"I know what I told you. I was a fool. I thought that I was doing you a favor by getting out of your life. I thought that your being involved with the Wulf could only hurt you and Emily." He released her, brought his hands up and cupped her face. "But I changed the day I opened that car door and found you. You changed me from an impenetrable creature who didn't want to leave his cave to a man who wants a life, wants to be known and wants to be loved."

Connie sighed, Molly's eyes filled with tears, and Wendy whispered, "If she doesn't kiss him right now, I will!"

April snorted. "Get in line."

"Goodnight, girls," Isabella said.

After her friends wished them both a Merry Christmas and made a quick exit, Isabella faced the man who made her see stars and spoke what was in her heart. "I love you, too, Michael. I've loved you…Lord, it seems like a lifetime. But I'm afraid to believe this."

"I know what it's like to be afraid, sweetheart," he said gently. "I spent most of my life that way, and I don't recommend it." A grin played about his lips. "You taught me how to love, Bella. And I won't let you go."

"You won't?"

"No. I'm no good without you."

Her heart squeezed painfully. "Are you sure?"

He snaked an arm around her waist and pulled her close. "Positive."

"Oh, Michael." Isabella looked up into his eyes and saw his soul, no mask, no wall—just a man in love—and she knew he was finally hers.

Grinning Michael pulled a sprig of mistletoe out of his pocket and held it between them. "Have I told you how much I love the holidays?" he asked as he lifted the mistletoe above their heads with one hand and pulled her closer with the other. He kissed her softly, then drew back, just far enough so she could feel his warm breath when he said, "You forgive me for being such an idiot?"

Tears welled up in her eyes and she could only nod.

"Then how about marrying me?"

Big fat tears that were directly attached to her heartstrings dropped onto her cheeks. "Say that again."

He grinned. "Marry me, Isabella Spencer?"

She smiled back. "In a heartbeat, Michael Wulf."

Lowering his head, he gave her a series of slow, tender kisses. "Come on. Let's go look in on our daughter."

For a moment she just stared at him, drinking in the man that he had finally allowed himself to liberate. He wanted them. He wanted a life with them. "Our daughter?"

"Oh, sweetheart, that little girl has been mine from the moment I first held her. And I can't wait to make it official, if you'll let me."

All of Isabella's dreams from so many Christmases past were coming true that Christmas Eve night. "Santa sure has come through this year."

Michael brushed his lips over hers, whispering, "Ho, ho, ho," before gently releasing her. "Let's go give our child a good-night kiss. We have a tree to decorate, stockings to hang and presents to wrap." He smiled and eased an arm around her. "My first traditions with the two people I love most in the world. What could be better?"

Smiling contentedly, Isabella let her head fall against his shoulder. "Nothing, Michael. Absolutely nothing."

Epilogue

Four years later...

Cotton-candy snow fell from the darkening sky onto the sidewalks, street lamps and jutting shop signs of Fielding. Anyone just passing through might have a great chuckle over the name on one of those signs, because it looked strangely like "The Wulf Fam Bakery" under that random coating of white. But to all who lived there, to all who had named it, they knew better. And every time they passed or entered the Wulf Family Bakery, they remembered the little miracle they'd witnessed all those years ago. When a lonely man had finally found his way home.

Just above the sign, behind a window on the second

floor, was a beautiful blue spruce. It's keepers were tending to it as though it were a member of the family, hanging lights, placing ornaments, flinging wisps of tinsel at its boughs.

And inside that home, under that tree, where so much warmth resided, sat Emily Wulf tearing open a present with the enthusiasm of a defensive lineman. After squealing with delight at the fuzzy-bear ornament she'd eyed at the Crafty Corner the other day, the little girl looked up at her father.

"Where should I put it, Daddy?"

Michael smiled down at his daughter, his heart. "Anywhere you like, princess."

And she truly was that, he thought. Emily was smart and kind and incredibly beautiful. She was her mother and yet...in some ways, she was him, too. Her stubbornness, her capacity for love.

"How 'bout by Annie's ornmant?" Emily said in her toddler speech.

Just at that moment, Bella walked into the room carrying their three-month-old baby girl. "I think putting it beside your sister's ornament is a wonderful idea, Ems."

Michael's heart tumbled at the sight of his wife.

Blue eyes shimmering, long blond hair loose and wispy around her face, Bella smiled first at Emily, then at him. She'd changed from her afternoon party clothes into that old blue robe he'd given her when she'd first come to stay with him. But what really took his breath away was the sight of her holding his child.

Emily tugged at his hand. "Up, Daddy."

With a chuckle Michael lifted her high in the air so she could place her ornament on the bough next to Annie's turtle figurine. This was Christmas Eve at Bella's old apartment—or what they now affectionately called their town house—and it was filled with traditions old and new. It was filled with warmth and love that soothed more than a wounded leg. And it was filled with something Michael Wulf had never expected to deserve: family.

After giving the tree a once-over, Bella deemed it perfection, then settled on the couch with Annie. Michael joined them, tugging Emily onto his lap.

"Can I say it, Daddy?" Emily asked.

Bella laughed and Michael just smiled. His eldest daughter was a *lot* like him. "All right."

Emily took a deep breath and shouted, "Light tree!"

In a blink, the blue spruce sparkled with white twinkling lights, and everyone who could talk oohed and aahed, just as they did every year.

Emily snuggled into the crook of his arm and said softly, "Tell the story."

Bella smiled at him, and he mouthed, "I love you."

This—this night of magic and decorating and dreams and Santa—was beyond wonderful. But the story Emily had asked to hear was a tradition that Michael himself had started.

The room was still and scented with pine. Michael

cuddled Emily close and began. ''The night that Emily Wulf came into the world, it snowed and snowed....''

*   *   *   *   *

*Look for Laura Wright's next red-hot
fiery tale in Silhouette Desire,*

CHARMING THE PRINCE,

in February 2003

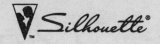

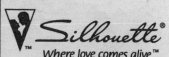

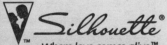

If you enjoyed what you just read,
then we've got an offer you can't resist!

Take 2 bestselling love stories FREE!
Plus get a FREE surprise gift!

COMING NEXT MONTH

SDCNM1202